NED AND THE CHOCOLATE CHEATS

Enjoy the
adventure.

(signature)

Ned

NED AND THE CHOCOLATE CHEATS

MARK JARVIS

Matador
9 Priory Business Park,
Wistow Road, Kibworth Beauchamp,
Leicestershire, LE8 0RX
Tel: 0116 279 2299
Email: books@troubador.co.uk
Web: www.troubador.co.uk/matador
Twitter: @matadorbooks

ISBN 978 1838591 793

British Library Cataloguing in Publication Data.
A catalogue record for this book is available from the British Library.

Printed and bound in the UK by TJ International, Padstow, Cornwall
Typeset in 12pt Minion Pro by Troubador Publishing Ltd, Leicester, UK

Matador is an imprint of Troubador Publishing Ltd

For Holly and Steffen,
who made the whole thing possible.

PROLOGUE

It was dark now. They saw their moment.

"Go!" Rufus shouted.

Crash!

Mrs Perkins' mobility scooter smashed into the shop window. It was not enough to break it completely, but weakened it for the pack of dogs to burst through. Broken glass tinkled and twinkled onto the ground around them.

The dogs furiously attacked the bars of chocolate on the shelves. Twelve sets of sharp teeth chomped and ate every one of them, including the wrappers. It all took seconds.

Now, as quickly as they had entered, the pack jumped out.

"I'm going to wish I hadn't eaten all that!" panted Scruff as he scampered away.

"Yeah," puffed Rufus frantically. "Especially when those tin foil wrappers come out again."

The dogs raced through the streets, splitting up to avoid detection. They were on their way to the next target, but would it be so easy?

CHAPTER 1
HEY, DUDE!

I stood at the back door. This is one of the ways I show people I want to go out to the garden.

The people think they are in charge, but who picks up my poop? Think about it! Dogs (especially handsome-looking, long-legged Jack Russell Terriers like me) are definitely in charge. Sort of.

The garden smelt good. I snuffled and sniffed the wall and the washing line post. They smelt nice and strongly of my wee. I weed on those places again to make sure others knew it was my garden.

I smelt another smell in the air and looked up. There she was, sitting on top of the stone wall.

"Morning, Gizzmo," I called.

"Hey, Ned, dude!" the cat replied.

Gizzmo, like most cats, thought of herself as a

cool surfer type. This is bonkers really, as most of them hate getting wet.

Cats like to behave in an 'awesome' and trendy way. I often saw Gizzmo hanging out in The Sticky Bun Café that I went past on my walks. Gizzmo could be seen with her Flat Bright animal coffee, writing something on her laptop. Now she was above me on the wall that separated our gardens.

"Did you catch the news about the sweet shop, dude?" she asked. As she spoke, she licked her paw and rubbed it over her ear.

"That's gross, Gizzmo, don't do that," I said.

"Gross? And this coming from a dude who sniffs bottoms!" she laughed.

"But no, Gizzmo, I didn't hear the news. What happened?"

She looked down at me. "Hey, you know that old dude, Mrs Perkins?"

"Yes," I said.

"Well, last night, a pack of street dog dudes drove that lady's mobility scooter through the sweet shop window. They stole all the chocolate! Most uncool."

"Wow!" I replied.

I sat down and scratched the side of my tummy. This was not particularly bad news for me, as chocolate is poisonous for animals. For the people, this was very bad. Not only was all that chocolate stolen, but it also meant that animals were now committing crimes. This was serious stuff.

I hoped the dogs who stole the chocolate didn't

eat it. Being a dog myself, I knew that they probably couldn't resist the urge to scoff it all.

"It's a doggy-dude ram-raid, dude!" Gizzmo chuckled.

"This is animal organised crime," I said. "It's a worrying thing. I need to tell my person about this."

Dogs and cats have been living in human company for thousands of years, so it was inevitable that they should learn to talk. It was bound to happen. Once the talking starts, it can lead to picking up all sorts of other human habits, good and bad. It didn't take long for many other animals to learn the skill of talking. Some are better at it than others. Some don't talk at all.

I looked up at the fluffy tabby cat, now stretched out in the sunshine. I tried to raise one eyebrow and appear serious. I couldn't do it and just looked like I had wind.

"Take a chill pill, dude," Gizzmo purred. "They were only after the chocolate." She went to sleep.

Scrambling to my feet, I turned towards the house. I sniffed the air and walked towards the smell of my person.

Being a Jack Russell, I am short and strong. I found it quite easy to nudge open the back door, which had closed a bit in the breeze. Once inside, I bounded across the room.

Jeff was sitting on the old leather sofa, reading a book. I jumped up next to him and pushed my nose up under his arm, to make sure I had his attention.

"What on earth...!" he exclaimed in surprise. "Ned, old pal, what's the matter?"

"Hey! Hey! Listen to this!" I shouted excitedly. I reached up and licked his face. Slurp!

Being able to talk didn't mean that I could stop myself doing dog things. He had the crumbs of this morning's breakfast still in his beard. Hmm, cornflakes! Nice.

"Yuk!" my person said, as he wiped his face on his sleeve. "Okay, you have my attention. Do try and sit still; you'll get hairs everywhere." Jeff scratched his tummy through his unironed t-shirt.

My person's proper name was Cornellius Jefferies, but that is rather a mouthful. Ever since he was at school, everyone had just called him Jeff. All that matters to me is that he is *my* person.

"Okay, Ned, this seems important," he smiled. "That will make a nice change!" As he grinned, his eyes twinkled behind his round glasses and he pushed back his unbrushed dark hair. *I do love you,* I thought. *But you are scruffy.*

People might shower every day, but I still look and smell better than them.

I stood up and shook, shedding little hairs everywhere, and then sat down again. Jeff brushed the hairs onto the floor.

"Listen," I said, trying to get to the point. "You know the sweet shop just down the road from here? The one that smells of liquorice? Well, Gizzmo, the cat that lives next door to us, told me that yesterday

4

evening, just as the shop was closing, the window was smashed and all the chocolate was stolen and eaten!" I said this quickly and stood up, my tail wagging in excitement.

"No way!" Jeff exclaimed. "But who would do such a thing?" He shrugged his shoulders.

"Ah, well, that's the really amazing part. It was a gang of dogs."

"Wow!" Jeff said in wonderment. "But isn't chocolate poisonous for dogs?"

"Yes. Dogs know that, but we just can't help eating it. It's the wonderful smell. It just smells so good!" I wagged my tail again at the thought of chocolate.

"You dogs are always thinking of your tummies," Jeff laughed. He picked up the remote control and flicked on the television that was fixed up on the wall. It came to life, showing one of the news channels.

I looked away and started on some serious self-grooming. It's important to always look your best, I think.

People like us to look good. Some of them spend a lot of time and money paying for us to be groomed. If we look good, they look good. It's just one of the many ways we help each other out. Mainly, though, we just like spending time in each other's company.

Cats, on the other hand, are different. Most of them only spend time with people when it suits them. Goodness knows what cats get up to at other times. Most other animals think it's better not to spend more time with humans than necessary.

"A *gang* of dogs, you say?" Jeff asked. He scratched the end of his nose in thought. "That means that they must have organised the crime themselves, doesn't it? Now I think you should look at this." With a flourish of his wrist like a magician, he pointed the remote control at the television and unpaused it from where he had been watching. It came on to the rolling news channel.

"Read the 'breaking news' that's going along the bottom of the screen. I know you are a good reader," he said, turning to me now as I sat beside him. "I saw you reading an article about ticks and fleas on my smartphone yesterday. By the way, how did you learn my passcode?" He raised a questioning eyebrow. "Never mind that now, though; look at the screen."

I read the line of sentences that was moving along the bottom of the television on a red bar. It said, *More mysterious chocolate robberies. Reports from around the country. Police baffled.*

"Well, what do you think of that?" Jeff asked, turning around to me again. "Gizzmo's story is just one of many. It's happening everywhere. Did the dogs organise the crime themselves, I wonder, or is someone organising them?"

I sat up smartly on the sofa. "Right!" I ordered. "Take me for a walk. I need to speak to other dogs and cats and find out what they know."

My person slowly got to his feet. Considering he ate so much, he still looked quite slim. I guess it was all the walks that I made him take me on that kept him so fit.

I jumped down onto the carpet, which was once a cream colour, and gave him my best 'you're not going out looking like that' look. He must have understood, because he mumbled something and disappeared for a few minutes. I sat and waited patiently. *There might be a biscuit in this for me*, I thought.

When Jeff returned, he was looking a lot smarter and smelling soapier. He said, "Ah, good boy!" and fed me a meaty-flavoured treat that he found in his pocket.

I tried to be still as he was putting on my lead, but the whole thing was getting so exciting!

"Okay," Jeff announced. "Are you ready...? Walkies!"

Jeff leaned over me to open the front door (I haven't yet worked out how I can open it by myself) and I pulled him out, down the short path and onto the street.

I think of my lead and harness as a safety belt. People wear safety belts in cars to keep them safe, if something unexpected happens. My lead is the same. For example, I might come across a really important smell that I have to investigate. I might not be able to think carefully as the smell takes me across a busy road.

You have to really concentrate on these smells, and you have to follow them wherever they go. Then wee on them, of course. I have to let everyone know I was there.

The worst is fast-moving things, as I just can't help myself. I have an uncontrollable urge to chase them!

Once again, my person keeps me safe, as I would even run out in front of the traffic to chase the fast thing, like a squirrel, for example.

I would not be a very good 'unaccompanied' animal. I'm not really sure what I would do if I caught up with the fast things. Growl and bark at them, I expect.

We walked out towards the local little café and bakery called The Sticky Bun, and turned right towards the sea. The sea was one of the good things about living in Plymouth; it was never far away and there was always a familiar salty smell in the air. It's nice to come back to if you've been away.

We turned off to the left and Jeff unclipped my lead as we were now walking along a bramble-hedged footpath. This leads down to Radford Park. Parks are super-duper smelly places!

I felt an overwhelming urge to just run off madly and poo somewhere, but not just anywhere. It had to be the right spot. It had to smell right.

When I'd finished and had a shake, I was feeling super satisfied. My person did his job and picked up my poo in a little plastic bag. Biodegradable plastic, of course. I insist on that.

"Right-ho!" I announced. "Just give me a few minutes and I'll see what I can find out."

"Okay," said Jeff, getting his smartphone out of his jeans pocket. "Good luck. Try not to get distracted."

I bounded off, following the smells to the nearest Bulldog. Bulldogs are often a great source of information. They might not be very active, but because they sit still they can do a lot of listening.

It didn't take me long. The Bulldog was sitting down next to a park bench on which his person was perched, talking to her friend on her phone.

"Hiya!" I said enthusiastically.

"Good morning," replied the large brown and white dog. His folds of floppy skin were moving up and down as he spoke. A pair of dog reading glasses hung on a chain around his neck.

"Brurr!" he snorted. "May I help you?"

I shook myself, with the usual flurry of hairs, and sat down in front of him.

There were a few other dogs and people walking around in the park, with a group of little people in shorts, kicking a ball to each other. Apart from that, the tweeting birds and the Bulldog's person on her phone, it was quite quiet.

"I just wanted to ask," I said, "have you heard about the pack of dogs stealing chocolate from the sweet shop?"

"Yes," he said slowly.

"Okay, good. Well, have you also heard that there are packs of dogs doing the same thing all over the country?"

"Yes."

"Oh, right!" I continued enthusiastically. "Well, Gizzmo the cat told me about our shop, and then when I told my person, he showed me that on the news it said that the police are baffled!" I said the whole thing quickly and the Bulldog took his time before answering.

"Yes," he agreed slowly.

"And I was wondering if you knew anything more about it?" He wasn't giving much away, this Bulldog.

"Yes," he replied, sliding his front legs forward until he was lying down on the grass.

"Is that yes, you do know something more about it? If you do, then could you tell me, please?"

"Yes." He paused and scratched his side with his back leg. I hoped that this was worth waiting for. He turned his big head to look at me.

"Do you know that the robberies all seem to have happened at a similar time, within a few hours of each other?" he asked. "And that they have all involved a stolen mobility scooter?"

"Well, that must mean they are all organised; they must all be planned," I answered. "How do you know all this?"

"It's my person," the Bulldog replied. "She talks a lot on her phone. Her friends who live in London have friends who have family and friends who live all over the place, and they have friends, and they all like to talk." He snorted again. "I just like to sit and listen."

"Wow! This is so exciting!" I stood up, looked around and sniffed the air, catching Jeff's smell. "Thank you, you've been very helpful!"

"Yes," he replied as I bounded off. I couldn't wait to tell my person.

CHAPTER 2
FLAT BRIGHT

"Really?" Jeff said as we walked back along the uneven surface of the flagstoned pavement, with little weeds growing in the cracks. "Now that information makes the idea of it being an organised crime seem even more sensible."

"Yeah!" I agreed, straining at my harness, feeling enthusiastic and wanting to get somewhere fast. Suddenly I stopped; there was a smell of another dog by the wall. The smell told me that it was quite a little dog. Quite an old dog too; the wee smelt like he had been licking the sweets called 'Humbugs'. We moved on.

"There is a lot more information to find out," I continued. "The police just say that they are 'baffled'. Does that mean that they have just given up?"

"Oh, look," said Jeff, not really listening to me. "Isn't that your mate Gizzmo?" He was indicating towards the window of The Sticky Bun. There was a fluffy tabby cat sitting at one of the tables, with what looked like a coffee and a silver-coloured Apple Mac laptop open in front of her.

"Yes, you're right," I replied, pulling towards the door. "I'd love a drink, thanks for asking! One of those 'Flat Bright' drinks like Gizzmo has, please."

Jeff groaned and we went into the coffee shop. I was pleased to see that the poster I'd asked to be put up in the window was still on display. It was a poster in support of better facilities for animals.

Most of us still live in the traditional way, with a person. There are a few animals now, though, who are living 'Unaccompanied'. This means they live by themselves or in a group, without a person. This is still quite hard to do, as if you don't have hands, you find it hard to do the simplest of tasks.

Living Unaccompanied or not, I feel strongly that there should be more facilities for animals. Some animals have jobs and pay taxes, so we have *rights*. I have recently written to Larry, the Number Ten Downing Street Cat, explaining my point of view. I have been collecting signatures and paw prints, for a petition.

Jeff unclipped me and sat me in the seat at the same table as Gizzmo.

"Hey, dude!" purred the cat. "The Flat Bright animal coffee is way cool in here. That barista is a talented coffee-making dude."

"What are you reading?" I asked. "Is it the news? 'Cos I found out some amazing stuff, from a Bulldog in the park." I paused as Gizzmo leaned over, closed her eyes and slowly sniffed her animal coffee, taking in the aroma.

"Can I just ask, though, Gizzmo, how do you get your laptop to the café and how do you pay all your Flat Bright animal coffee bills?"

"That's easy, dude," she replied with a chuckle. "My person carries the laptop over here for me. We've gotta little account running at the café, which she pays off every couple of weeks.

She says that she would rather know where I was, than just wandering the streets. Dude, anything could happen out there! This suits me just fine."

"That sounds like a *puuur*fect arrangement!" I agreed. My cat jokes are great.

Jeff returned with the drinks and a rather grumpy expression on his face. He put them down on the table in front of us and sat down. Undoing the zip on his coat, he said, "No wonder we don't come in here very often. Do you know how much these cost me?"

"Hey, you gotta pay for quality, dude!" said Gizzmo.

"Hmm," Jeff mumbled. "Why do you animals always drink those Flat Bright animal coffees anyway?"

"One, they are always served in these low, wide sort of cups," I answered. "Watch."

Both Gizzmo and I simultaneously leant forward and started lapping at the froth on top of the coffees.

"You just try lapping out of one of those tall latte glasses, dude!" exclaimed Gizzmo. "It's like major face froth, even if you've gotta long tongue."

We all stopped and watched a tall and slim Weimaraner dog-waiter delicately manoeuvre around the tables. She had four hot chocolates on a tray, which was fixed to a harness on her back.

"And two," I continued, "normal coffee and tea have a chemical called caffeine in them, which is really bad for cats and dogs. These special Flat Bright drinks have no caffeine. They are creamy and frothy and help to keep our teeth clean and bright!" Gizzmo and I grinned, showing our white teeth.

"Anyway," I said, becoming serious, sitting up and slipping a little bit on the shiny surface of the seat, "these chocolate robberies, they are happening everywhere. Like I said, it's organised crime."

"So you keep saying," said Jeff, leaning forward so that both of his arms rested on the crowded tabletop. He looked behind him over both shoulders, to check if anyone else was in earshot, and then lowered his voice, so that only we could hear. "But organised by whom?"

CHAPTER 3
SEND ME A TEXT

"Welcome to Bohol!" shouted the tour guide warmly, greeting the tourists as they stepped from the bobbing ferry onto the wooden slats of the landing stage. "Welcome to the home of the famous Chocolate Hills and the beautiful tarsier monkey!"

The small group of visitors were a variety of ages, animals and nationalities. They had a range of luggage with them. The tourists trundled, hobbled or strode jauntily from the wooden pier onto the firm, dry, earthy patch of land. The tour guide stood waiting for them.

"Hey, guys, my name is Christian!" he said in an American accent, his voice as loud as his eye-wateringly bright patterned shirt.

The tourists now stood around him, their bags resting on the earth or on tufts of grass in the clearing.

Christian continued, "Bohol is one of the many beautiful islands of the Philippines. You will be able to see fabulous tropical plants and wildlife, and if you are very lucky, you will be able to see our famous and endangered beautiful little Bohol monkeys, called tarsiers."

There were a few cheers from the younger members of the party and some smiles from the adults accompanying them.

"Yeah, guys!" smiled Christian. "So I will now take you to your fabulous hotel, if you all just follow me this way."

In a leafy, shady tree, just overlooking the spot where the group came ashore, a little tarsier watched the tourists. Being nocturnal, he was now feeling very sleepy in the sunlight of midday. The tarsier's huge eyes blinked slowly and he heard the chatter of the visitors for a long time as they walked away. They soon left him and his lofty spot quiet again.

He gripped the branch that he was sitting on, and his furry arm now reached behind him for his smartphone, wedged into a fork in the branches. The tarsier's head turned one hundred and eighty degrees around as he again read the text message he had received.

Party of twenty-five tourists arriving at 12pm today, it said.

Holding the phone with his other foot, he wrote a text reply, his long fingers tapping over the keys.

They're here now. Thanx for info, homey. I'll get back 2 ya.

It was very tiring being a tough criminal mastermind; it was way past his bedtime. Anyway, little tarsiers need plenty of sleep, and this little tarsier needed to dream of his next dastardly scheme.

CHAPTER 4
VOMIT

I sniffed at the smell of wee that was low down on the leg of the park bench on which my person sat. He leaned back with his arms folded and his eyes closed, enjoying the winter sunshine.

"What are you doing, Ned?" he asked. "You've been sniffing at that spot for ages now."

"Yes, hang on," I replied between sniffs. "What you people don't get is that there is a lot of information in these smells." I stopped sniffing and jumped up next to him. "You see," I continued, in a flurry of little white hairs that I shook out before I settled down, "this smell is different. It's quite fresh but it is very sweet, almost chocolatey. The most unusual thing is, whoever did it, is not a well dog."

"You *can* tell a lot by a smell, and I just thought

you were doing disgusting dog things. How fresh do you think it is?" Jeff enquired, not moving from his sun-worshipping position.

"Very fresh," I replied firmly. "Weed today, recently."

"So that dog could still be here in the park?"

I was already off the bench and sniffing for smells. I saw what Jeff was suggesting. They might still be here.

"Have you seen a… dog that smells chocolatey?" I asked a springy Whippet as she skipped past with her person.

"You said that the cute little Pug we saw smelt funny," offered her person helpfully, bending down to straighten the Whippet's fancy leather collar.

"Get off, don't fuss!" shrugged the Whippet. "Yes, he did smell funny, but that's because the Pug's person had sprayed him with that awful doggy perfume!"

"Shame," I said. "That's just not right, is it? Well, thanks for your help."

She trotted on in her direction and I in mine.

I stopped and sniffed the air near an area of bushes. There was that smell again. But this time it was stronger and mixed with a sickly aroma.

Then I heard it. A soft dismal grown from inside the bush. I decided to go in and investigate. I pushed the branches aside with my strong nose and forced my way through twigs and brambles. I stopped still. There was that sound again, but a lot louder. I was going in the right direction.

I burst through into a small clearing. There was a big German Shepherd, looking most bedraggled. He was lying on his side by a pile of his own sick.

"Ooh!" he groaned. "Help!"

I rushed over, quickly taking in that the sick had glittery silver bits in it. The poor dog had obviously been here for a couple of days.

"My goodness!" I cried. "Umm… stay here," I said stupidly. "I'll go and get help."

I left the dog groaning and rushed back out of the path that I had forged through the bushes. I ran to my person. Jeff was still sitting on the bench with his arms folded and his eyes closed, but this time he was snoring.

I jumped up beside him again and poked my nose under his arm to wake him.

"Wha… wha… what? What is it?" He put his hand down onto the bench and turned to me.

"Quick!" I panted. "I found the funny-smelling dog and he's not well. Come quick! This looks bad."

Jeff grumbled a bit and slowly got to his feet. "Okay, lead the way," he said.

I scampered ahead across the grass, stopping and turning now and again so that my person could catch up.

"It's all right for you," he puffed. "You have four-wheel drive."

"Come on, slowcoach!" I called. "We're nearly there."

I easily pushed through the bushes again, now that I knew my way. Jeff was not quite as quick, having to brush aside tangled branches and twigs.

Eventually, we both reached the clearing. The funny-smelling dog was still there, lying on his side and groaning.

"Oh dear!" exclaimed Jeff, kneeling down beside the distressed German Shepherd. "You don't look at all well, poor thing. I think I'm going to have to try and carry you to our vets. I bet they will have you as right as rain in no time."

"No!" gasped the funny-smelling dog. "No vets, please!" He gasped his pleas from the ground, barely lifting his head. "They'll ask questions… and then the police will be involved. It can't happen… ohhh!"

"Well, you feel cold," observed Jeff, laying his hands on the German Shepherd's head and side. "And I'm not a vet, so you need some expert help. Wait a minute… what's that silvery stuff in your sick?" Jeff was staring at the sick, which was all around the ill dog. "That looks like bits of tin foil, quite a lot of it too."

"Yes," I said, standing next to them and taking a sniff of the German Shepherd and then the sick. "I have a theory. Sweet smell, ill dog, sick and tin foil. Have you been eating a bar of chocolate with the wrapper still on it?"

The sick dog said nothing at first; he just groaned again. Then he said, "Not just one… lots of bars. Different sorts of chocolates… and eating them very quickly. I had to… to complete my mission and to prove that I am a true believer."

"Believer in what?" Jeff and I both exclaimed.

"Surely you know that chocolate is poisonous for dogs?" I added.

The German Shepherd paused again, maybe for dramatic effect. "A believer in Gabâ!" he said at last with great solemnity. "The Great Gabâ! The one true spirit that will save animals from the evil of humans!"

"Wow," I said at last, feeling very surprised. "Well, perhaps he will pay your vet bills too. Can you lift him… 'evil' human?" I joked with my person. "You can tell us more on the way to the vets," I said to the dog.

Jeff crouched and wriggled his hands under the German Shepherd until he was able to cradle him in his arms. He stood up straight again. "By the way, what's your name?" he asked as he carefully pushed backwards, out of the bushes and into the park.

"Rufus," the dog replied quietly.

"Well, Rufus," I said as I walked beside them, "I think I've got a few questions for you."

We eventually got Rufus home and into the car. He lay on the back seat under a blanket and I sat up next to him.

"Let me get this straight," I said. "You are telling us that this 'Great Gabâ', whom you've never met, sent his messenger to tell you that by breaking into a newsagent's with your gang and eating all of the chocolate, you are doing his work, to save animals?"

"Yes," Rufus replied. He was feeling a little better, now that Jeff had given him a drink. He was feeling warmer too, under an old green blanket that we kept in the boot for emergencies.

"I've been living on the street for a while now," he continued. "I joined a street gang of other homeless dogs for protection. I was abandoned as a puppy and have had to fend for myself. It's dangerous out there."

"Yes, I understand. I'm really lucky to have such a good home. But why the robbery and the chocolate?"

Rufus shifted uncomfortably before he answered. "The messenger is offering us a good future. He told us about the Great Gabâ who looks after all animals. He told us that we are on the streets because humans are cruel to us. He told us that to show our support to the one that really looks after us, we need to do his work. We need to make humans unhappy, the way that they have made us unhappy. We need to destroy all their chocolate."

"Even if it means making yourself ill?" I asked, amazed by this unbelievable idea.

I could see from looking out of the window, leaving a little smear where my wet nose rubbed, that we were quite near to the vets.

"Yes. Only Gabâ's faithful followers would risk themselves in that way," Rufus murmured dreamily.

"And that's what the messenger told you?" I replied. "Wow. I guess you have to feel really desperate to believe that."

We pulled up at the vets and Jeff opened the back door to pick up Rufus. I jumped down onto the pavement.

"Please don't say anything to the vet!" pleaded Rufus.

"We won't," Jeff said, staggering up the steps and through the vets' swing doors. "I'll say I left a bar of chocolate on the floor and you couldn't resist it. They wouldn't believe your story anyway."

The vet took the stethoscope out of her ears and allowed the two earpieces to spring back around her neck.

"I'm sure he will be absolutely fine now," she said, smiling at everyone. "From what you describe to me, he's got rid of all the tin foil from the wrapper and there doesn't seem to be any damage done. But chocolate can be poisonous for dogs, especially in large quantities…"

At this, Rufus' eyes met mine and once again I attempted to raise an eyebrow.

"…but his temperature is within the normal range now and the fluids that he has taken on board will soon help to flush everything out." She smiled again, unpeeled the surgical rubber gloves from her hands and pushed the small, thin glasses back onto her nose. "You've been a very lucky dog!" she said to Rufus.

Rufus just groaned in reply.

"Well, just take it easy for a couple of days and try to eat simple, plain food, like rice or scrambled egg, or plain cooked chicken. Okay?" she said, concluding our consultation.

Rufus rolled over from his side and onto his feet. My person lifted him down from the vet's table and onto the floor. Rufus shook himself and stood a little unsteadily.

"Thanks!" Jeff called to the vet as we made our way out. "We'll make sure he rests."

Jeff paid the vet's bill to the receptionist. As we made our way down the steps to the pavement, Rufus looked at us sheepishly.

"Thanks. Thanks, both of you. You saved my life." He paused and then said very seriously, "I know that Gabâ in his greatness thanks you too. Now I may serve him again another day."

"Oh no!" I said, feeling annoyed. "Not that nonsense again. Just get in the car quickly and let's work out what we are going to do with you."

"I must go back and join my gang," Rufus insisted. He was slowly moving away from us as we stood on the pavement with the car door open.

"No, surely not!" Jeff exclaimed. "Don't you want to change your life now you have a chance? We'll help you."

"No, I must go," insisted Rufus. "I have sworn a solemn oath to my gang. We all have. They will come looking for me if they know I am alive and have not returned. I must go. Goodbye. Gabâ be with you!"

Rufus disappeared down a footpath next to the vets. In a second, he was gone from our sight.

"Well," said Jeff as we got into the car, "this whole story just gets stranger and stranger."

"Yes," I agreed. "What started off as a break-in at our local newsagent's quickly turned into a country-wide organised crime story." I paused to bark at a passing postman. "And to make things worse, it seems like these gangs of dogs have been sort of 'brainwashed' into believing that they are doing the work of some individual called Gabâ."

Jeff nodded in agreement. I carried on ranting. "And to top it all, Gabâ wants the dogs to put themselves at risk to prove that they are loyal to him. It just doesn't make sense."

"Hmm…" pondered Jeff as he drove us home. "What's it all about and why aren't the authorities doing something? I don't know about you, but I've got an uneasy feeling. Something big is going to happen."

CHAPTER 5
ROAD TRIP

The next day, Jeff and I were packing to drive to London to stay with Jeff's sister, Finulla Jefferies. Cornellius and Finulla's parents thought that it would be cool and different to give their children unusual names. Cornellius and Finulla had their own opinions on that.

Finulla, or 'Noola', as she was known to her friends, lived in an area of London called Shoreditch. I always liked going there as there was lots of fun to be had and interesting things to see.

I wanted to get to London by taking the train. I like going on the train, but Jeff explained how much more that would cost us.

"Besides," he said, "in the car, we can stop and get out for a wee and we can travel from door to door."

I went out for a sniff and a wee in the back garden before we left, and to see Gizzmo, who was out sitting on the garden wall, enjoying the sunshine.

"Hey, Ned, dude!" called Gizzmo.

"Hello, Gizzmo," I replied cheerfully. "We're going up to London this morning, but we can keep in contact with video calls through my person's smartphone and your laptop."

"Yeah, great idea! We need to keep in contact in case anything else happens in this weird chocolate mystery. What you told me about that dog Rufus and his gang was super strange. I'm going to check out this crazy 'Gabâ' dude on the net."

"Yes, please, Gizzmo. Let me know what you find out."

"Yo, Neddy, check out the far corner of your garden, by the shed. It looks like there's a pair of Jeff's underpants that have blown off the washing line."

I bounded over to investigate. There was indeed a pair of underpants, but they weren't Jeff's. They didn't smell like his. They were orange, rather shredded and tatty. I gave them a poke with my nose.

"Gizzmo, look!" I called. "There is something written on them. Do you think it might be a message?"

Gizzmo acrobatically climbed around the garden wall to be above me. She leant down to have a look. "Hey, it might be a message thrown over your wall. I don't think I noticed it earlier, dude. Read it out."

I circled round the underpants until the writing was the right way up. "It's written in pen," I remarked.

"Terrible handwriting. Maybe a dog wrote it. Umm… Let me see… Wow, it says, *Danger of Death. Keep Away*."

"Wowzers, dude!" exclaimed Gizzmo. "Those are some scary underpants. Do you think it's meant for you? Or is it just a warning about the state of the underpants?"

"I'm not sure, Gizzmo, but I'm very glad we are going away for a few days. I want to leave all this strange stuff behind me. I don't like it one bit."

"Sure thing, dude," said Gizzmo. "You two need to go away and relax."

"I'll try. See you soon!" I called. "I'm going to pretend I never saw them."

I had one quick last wee before we left and bounded back into the house.

Jeff was just lugging his suitcase down the stairs. I told him about the message but he wasn't very concerned. "It'll just be children mucking about," he said. "You ready, Ned? Then let's go!"

The journey from Plymouth to London took us about five hours, with only one wee-stop. The traffic only started to get heavy as we approached the busy capital city.

My person parked the car and unclipped my dog seatbelt. I jumped down onto the pavement and had a good scratch, first one side and then the other.

Wearing my dog seatbelt always felt a bit itchy. We were on a street of terraced houses with their front doors opening onto the pavement. There was a great smell here that I really needed to check out.

A yellow door opened and out stepped Jeff's sister, Finulla, to help us with our bags and welcome us in. She had been cooking and rubbed her hands down the front of her white apron.

"Hi, you guys!" she called. "Did you have a good journey, Ned?" She gave Jeff a big hug and bent over to fondly rub my ears, pulling her dangling ponytail to one side.

"Yes, thank you," I answered. "The traffic was good and it didn't take too long. I'm dying for a wee, though; may I use your back garden, please?"

"Sure, help yourself; the back door is open."

"Thanks," I replied and made my way through the house, through to the kitchen and out to the backyard.

Noola didn't really have a back garden like we did at home in Plymouth. It was more of a yard with raised flowerbeds all around the outside. It was surrounded by a high stone wall.

There were no dog smells in the yard but there were the odd smells of passing cats, who had been crossing from one yard to the next.

I weed against one of the flower beds, but as I finished, I had a funny feeling that someone was watching me. I raised my head to quickly glance around at the tops of the walls.

I froze. Was that a finger that was just over the top of the stone work? Looking again carefully, I could see it was only a twig. It must be my imagination. *You are seeing dangers where there are none*, I told myself. Those underpants had rattled me, though. It might be more than just kids. "We are quite safe in Noola's house," I said out loud. Weren't we?

CHAPTER 6
ON HER MAJESTY'S SECRET SERVICE

"Now that we're all unpacked, I'm just going to take Ned out for a quick run around in that little park you have at the end of your street," Jeff said to his sister. He turned to me and said, "I expect you would like to stretch your legs, Ned?"

"Yes, please," I replied, glad that he asked. "And I can check out some new smells too!"

"Okay, boys," Noola agreed. "I'll sort out a bite to eat for when you come back."

We went out onto the pavement again, carefully closing the yellow wooden door behind us. After Jeff had checked there was no traffic, I scampered across to the small park that sat like an island in the middle of a square of other terraced houses. The park, known as Jesus Green, was surrounded by black metal railings, and we entered through a squeaky gate.

As soon as I was on the grass, I felt a spurt of energy and I ran across to the other side as fast as I could. I had a quick smell of the railings and sprinted back again.

"Wow, that's better," I said to Jeff. "I needed that."

"I bet you did," Jeff replied. "I'm just going to sit down on that wooden bench in the middle. Come over and join me when you've had a run around."

"All righty," I called as I made my way along the railings at the side. There were exciting smells here of all sorts of different dogs, cats and humans. I weed on everything I could. This was going to be a really interesting park! Although I hadn't expected it to be quite as interesting as it turned out to be.

When I had finished and made my way back to my person, I saw that there was someone else also sitting on the bench. It was obviously a man, with shiny black shoes and black trousers. I couldn't see his body or face because of a large newspaper that he was holding up in front of him. His black gloved hands were holding the newspaper, and the top of his smart black Homburg-style hat was sticking up out of the top.

I jumped up next to Jeff, in between him and the man with the newspaper. I shook myself, letting fly the usual cloud of white hairs.

Jeff pressed his lips tightly together in a sort of smile, as he saw that many of the hairs had landed on the trouser leg of the man with the newspaper.

Suddenly I jumped as the stranger spoke from behind his newspaper.

"Don't look at me as I speak to you; look at each other, as if you are having a conversation. We are being watched," the man behind the newspaper said, in a slightly whispered but clear and careful voice. He sounded posh and very efficient. All the time he spoke whilst he was hidden by his newspaper, so we didn't see who he was.

I turned to face Jeff as instructed. The man continued.

"I know who you chaps are. I know all about you. I know that you are called Ned and Cornellius. You have both travelled here from Plymouth today. We are from the Secret Intelligence Service, MI5 to you, and we know everything."

"Ooh!" I said, but facing towards Jeff, as the man had asked. "*We*, you say? Who else is there?" He did not reply. There was an uncomfortable moment of silence.

"Well," I continued, "pleased to meet you."

"Yes," said the man behind the newspaper. "Likewise. As I said, we know everything and we know that you know something we have known about for a while, that we know that you can tell us about."

"Erm…" said Jeff slowly, sounding a little confused. "But I thought you said that you know everything?"

"We do," the man behind the newspaper replied. "We want to know how much you know. For instance, what is the name of the dog that you took to the vets? The one who ate all the chocolate with the wrappers still on? Who told him to do it? We want to know who delivered the underpants message and who controls the dog gangs and lastly, who is Gabâ?" His newspaper shook as he spoke, as if to emphasise the importance of what he said. "Don't look at me!" he hissed. "We are being watched!"

"How do you know all this?" I asked. I had turned to face him as he was speaking and turned quickly back again.

"That information is given on a need-to-know basis only. We need answers quickly and you have been able to get closer to a gang member than anyone. You are a dog, so they trust you. We need you chaps to find out more for us."

"Uh, okay," I said. "But how?"

"Just carry on doing what you are doing. Yes, as you were. But stay alert and be careful. There will be dangers for both of you. Now look here, when I stand up, I will leave a parcel for you on the bench. Pick it up. Don't open it until you are inside. It contains all of the things you will need to follow the trail and find out more. Good luck, you are working for your country now. The Royal Corgis and their person, The Queen, expect every animal to do its duty!"

With that, he stood up. Still holding the newspaper in front of him, he made his way out of the park, through one of the gates and into a black London taxi that had just pulled up. It drove off straight away.

My person and I just looked at each other in sheer amazement and then both turned to look at the brown paper package that the man had left on the park bench. Jeff's hand shot out and he picked it up, hiding it under his coat.

We turned our heads to look carefully around the outside of the park to see who was watching us. We saw no one, although it's possible we were being watched from the windows of any of the terraced houses.

Making our way back, both of us were eager to find out what had been left for us inside the package. Jeff knocked on the yellow door of Noola's house.

She opened it with a broad smile. "Hello, you two, you're just in time. Come in, I've set the table. Just sit down and I'll bring you some of my homemade soup!"

The smell was delicious and I almost forgot all about the package. One of the chairs was pulled out already and I jumped up onto it.

Jeff sat down opposite to me. He had taken his coat off but he still held onto the brown package. He put it down in an empty space on the wooden tabletop.

Exciting-smelling, thick, creamy pea and ham soup filled the bowls that were put down in front of us. I patiently watched the steam rising as Noola brought in her own soup. She placed a big bowl of crusty bread rolls in the middle of the table and then sat down.

"Well!" she said. "Dig in, before it gets cold. Ned, be careful before you stick your tongue into that soup; make sure it has cooled down enough. Now whatever do you have there in that package?" Noola looked down at the parcel, lying there invitingly.

"You may well ask," Jeff replied. "It was given to us by a man in the park, reading a newspaper. He said that Ned and I knew a lot about those chocolate robberies that have been happening all over the country. He wanted us to find out more."

"How very strange," Noola remarked. "Did he say who he was?"

"He said he was from MI5," I answered, though unable to take my eyes from the soup, trying to make it cool down with my willpower. "He said that the package contained things that we might find useful."

"MI5!" Noola exclaimed. "They are the spies that deal with secret security things. They work from that big building that you can see next to the River Thames. Or is that MI6? I can never tell the difference. You'd better open it then."

Jeff plonked the package in the space next to the bowl of crusty bread and began to tear open the brown paper wrapper.

"Oh, wow!" he said. "You guys are not going to believe this." He had seen a glimpse of the contents from the piece he had torn open. Now he fully tore the package, and its secrets spilled out onto the table.

The first thing I noticed was banknotes. There were lots of banknotes, hundreds of pounds of many different denominations and from different countries. They were all held together with an elastic band, and tucked under the band, on top of the pile, was a plastic credit card. It was a black AMEX card with a handwritten sticky note on it that said, *This card has no spending limit. Don't go mad with it.*

Secondly, I noticed four little maroon-coloured books. They had the British coat of arms on the cover. They were passports. *But why four?* I wondered.

The third thing I noticed was a smartphone. It suddenly began to vibrate and ring.

"Quick! One of you, answer it!" I exclaimed.

Jeff made a grab for it and saw that it was a video call. He turned around a bit in his seat and held the phone up so that we could all see it.

At first, on the screen, it just looked like a newspaper. Then the picture pulled back to reveal the man who was on the bench. This time, though, he sat in a plain white room but he still held the newspaper up in front of him. Only his legs, black gloved hands and the top of his hat were visible.

"Hello again," he said. "Oh, time for tea, eh! Terribly sorry, won't take long. This phone indicated to me that you had opened the package and it was time to call you. It has a tracking device inside it. Let me explain further. The money is for you to use to fund your operation. You have been tasked to find out more about the gangs of dogs stealing chocolate, and this Gabâ character. You will need money to travel; for taxis, for petrol, for train fares and, we suspect, for aeroplane fares. Then you will also need to pay for hotels and also perhaps for other things…" He paused and we all considered what these other things might be.

I took this opportunity to ask, "But why are there four passports? Is someone else coming?"

"No," he replied. "It's just you two, Ned. Have you looked inside them yet? Go on, have a look now."

Noola scooped up the passports and looked inside at the pages that showed our photographs and all of our identification details.

"But…" she stammered, "I don't understand. These two are obviously Ned's and my brother's." She put two of the passports to one side. "But these two…"

"Look carefully at the photographs, read the names, and look again at the things that are in the package."

"Well, this one is a human, so I guess this is to do with you," she said to Jeff. "Except in the picture is a person that looks a bit like you, but they have a clean-shaven chin, no beard, no glasses and they have a large moustache. And the name is someone else's. It's 'John Smith.'"

"Yes, and the other one, the dog…" the man behind the newspaper said.

"Okay," said Noola. "This one looks a bit like you, Ned. Except the dog is a Golden Retriever sort of colour and also has a large moustache! This dog is called 'Nedmondo'. Now that's just silly!" Noola put down the passport, folded her arms and pulled an incredulous face at the man behind the newspaper.

"Not at all," he said. "If you are going to have convincing disguises, then you must not stray too far from the truth. You will also find in the package two false moustaches, some contact lenses to replace the glasses and some Golden Retriever-coloured hair dye. You two might be going to some dangerous places, and it will be necessary to change your identities."

"John Smith, though," groaned Jeff.

"You might be surprised how many people there are in the French Foreign Legion who have changed their identities to John Smith. It's very popular amongst English people. Now, you can always contact me through this phone; it is a secure line. As I am your Handler, it is to me only that you report. Don't be fooled into telling anyone else anything. Except the cat, Gizzmo. She is very clever and will be able to help you. She'll do a lot of research for you. Jolly good. That's everything. Goodbye and good luck."

With that, the phone went dead and once again we all sat and looked at each other.

"Well, you had better all eat your soup before it's completely ruined," Noola said, rather grumpily. "Nedmondo and John indeed."

CHAPTER 7
BURIED

After we had eaten our delicious lunch, Noola said that as she had some things that she had to do that afternoon, why didn't we go and explore the local area? Today was Sunday and Columbia Road flower market was just close. We weren't very far from Brick Lane, which would also be very busy today. There would be lots of street food vendors and so there would be great smells and sights.

We made our way past the little park and into the busy throng of the bustling flower market. The street was closed off to traffic and was packed with people and flower stalls. The market traders were calling out to attract customers. "Two bunches for a pound! Now you won't find a deal better than that!"

It was difficult to walk in between all the people's

legs, and I was glad that Jeff put my lead on or else we would quickly have become separated. The smell of all the wonderful flowers was really strong, but even so, I managed to sniff out a few other dogs. I spotted another Jack Russell, sitting in a quiet spot beside one of the flower stalls, whilst his person bought some fresh flowers.

"All right, son?" he greeted me as I edged past.

"Yes, thanks!" I replied. "It's really busy and crowded today, isn't it?"

"Oh, yeah," the Jack Russell agreed. "It's like this when there's a market on, innit? Keep a close eye on your person now! You don't wanna get lost!"

"I will, thanks, bye!" I said cheerfully.

We moved on through the crowd and out to the end of the road, where it was a little quieter.

"Now my sister said that we should just go through here… oh, wait. I think the 'spy' phone is ringing!" Jeff reached into a pocket inside his jacket and pulled out the spy phone. "Oh no, it's my other phone." He shoved it back again and pulled out his own device. "Hello, Gizzmo!" he exclaimed, as he swiped across the slider on the screen to answer the video call.

"Bend down a bit," I called up to him. "I want to speak to her too."

My person crouched down so that we could both see the screen. Gizzmo's fluffy face came into view. I could see from the picture that she was sitting at a table in the coffee shop.

"Hey, dudes!" she greeted us. "How's it hanging?"

"Yes, we're good, thanks," I answered before Jeff could get a word in. "I'm glad you phoned because I've got something quite extraordinary to tell you."

As we sat there on the pavement (I sat, my person crouched), I quickly told Gizzmo all that had happened in Jesus Green that morning.

"Whoa, that's so cool," said Gizzmo. "You guys are like real spies or something."

"And you as well, Gizzmo," I said. "The man behind the newspaper said that we should keep in contact with you, as you are great at research."

"That is so way cool," Gizzmo replied. "Just tell me what you want me to do, dudes."

"Nothing yet," Jeff said. He moved himself back a little from the edge of the pavement as someone came past with another large trolley full of flowers.

"I'm not even sure what *we* are supposed to be doing," I explained. "The man behind the newspaper said that we should just stay alert."

"Well, I'm here if you need me, dudes. I'll track you as you move around using this cool app called 'Poodle Maps'. Stay in touch!" With that, Gizzmo rang off and Jeff stuffed the phone back into his jeans pocket.

"Get your phone out again," I said. "You can use the maps app so that we don't get lost."

"Good idea," Jeff replied. "I'd forgotten all about that. Okay, the map says that Brick Lane is… this way!"

I got up onto my feet, had a quick shake and a wee against the wall (just so that people would know I'd been there) and followed along on the pavement.

The streets began to get busier again, and the smells of different types of cooking became stronger and stronger. As we walked into the sea of people's legs, I caught amazing yummy aromas, both from the street vendors and from the bits of food and litter that had fallen to the floor. I loved all the busyness. These streets always made me feel that something exciting was about to happen.

"This is Brick Lane here," Jeff said. "Look at the old cobbles and the shop fronts. Imagine one of these barber shops could be Sweeney Todd's barbers! We could be made into pies!" he said, in a pretend scary voice.

"Oh, that sounds mysterious. I'll have to find out about that when we get home."

I pulled towards another smell that I wanted to explore. I didn't feel the comfortingly familiar tug on my collar of the lead that kept us close together. I looked back around towards my person.

My lead wasn't attached anymore. It was just lying limply on the cobbled street. It had been cut about fifty centimetres along, from where it joined my collar.

There was no sign of Jeff on the end of it.

In a fraction of a second, all the sights, smells and sounds disappeared, to be replaced by the musty smell of a thick, heavy sack.

CHAPTER 8
COAL HOLE

The sack had been pulled over my head and I felt myself being scooped up into it and carried into the air. There was a bump against my side as I was slung onto somebody's back. I was jogged about quickly; we were moving. There were muffled voices and the slam of a heavy door.

It all happened so quickly I hadn't time to think about what to do, but after more jostling I was dropped down onto a hard surface. Jeff's words about being made into pies suddenly came back to me as the top of the sack went limp. There was another slam of the door and everything was still.

I carefully poked my head up out of the sack and looked around.

I remember that when I was a pup, my parents

told me that if ever I felt unsure of a situation, the first thing I should do was to stay still and find out as much information as possible, before doing anything.

It was dark; I could see nothing.

As my nose came clear of the rough material, I started sniffing. I could smell a number of things. First, the room I was in had a damp scent like old fireplaces. It had a coal aroma, a bit like the chimneys of our old terraced house at home. I could also sniff out faint cooking smells and the distinctive pong of people and dogs.

What could I hear? Well, nothing clearly, but I was definitely aware of the sound of voices. I could not make out the words that they were using, but only sense the murmur of conversation.

I carefully shook off the sack and stepped out to stand on the stone floor. It had a cold, gritty feel.

Suddenly I spun around to face a blinding white light as the heavy door was swung open again. Something tall and large was shoved in by unseen hands and the door was slammed shut.

The big sack hit the floor with a large thud and I heard a loud voice that I recognised. "Oh, flippin' heck!" it grumbled loudly. It was the unmistakable voice of my person!

"Hang on, keep still a minute," I said. "I'll help you out."

I grabbed at the sack and wrestled with it, until I had pulled it clear of Jeff's head.

"Wow! It's dark in here!" he exclaimed. "I can't see a thing. Where are we, Ned? What just happened?"

"As for where we are, I have no more idea than you have. But I think it's quite clear that we have been kidnapped! I still think that they are quite close by because I can hear voices. Hey, haven't you got a torch on your phone?"

"Yes, I have," Jeff confirmed, "but it was snatched from my hand before they pulled the sack over my head. I was using Poodle Maps, remember?"

"What about the other phone? The spy one; did they take that?"

"You are brilliant, Ned! I'd forgotten all about that one."

Jeff reached inside his jacket once again and pulled out the phone that we had been given that morning. He flicked on the torch and at last we could see that we were shut in an old, empty cellar. It was grubby and dirty with black dust.

"Okay," I said. "You can phone for help now."

"Good plan, Ned, but no, I can't. There is no signal down here."

"Well, what's that up there in the corner? Shine your torch up there."

In the torchlight, we could see it was a small square metal grate.

"Lift me up there, will you?" I asked. "That's where I think the conversation I can hear is coming from. Hold me near the grate so that I can hear properly."

I could indeed hear better, and what I heard almost made me wish that I'd stayed on the ground.

One voice, a deep growl with a strong cockney accent, said, "Well, boss, what do we do now? We got 'em like you said, and they're safe in the old coal cellar."

"*Si*, yes!" said a higher posh sort of voice. It had the rhythm of an Italian accent. "Now will-a you get one of your 'umans to lift me and put-a me down on top of the table, so dat I can talk to you all?"

That must be the dog that I could smell. It sounded like he might be in charge.

He continued, "De instructions dat I was-a given, were to eliminate dem as soon as is possible. Dose two, dey know-a too much already. Dat-a stupid dog who raided one of de newsagents in Plymuff, 'as given away too much of our information. It's a shame dat-a eating all dat chocolate doesn't-a kill him. We 'ave sent dem a warning wid-a de underpants, so now it is only fair dat we 'ave-a de permanent solution."

"'Ow we gonna 'do' vem in, boss?" said another voice. "Just tell me an' I'll do it now!"

"Now wait-a just a minute," the Italian-voiced boss said firmly. "De Great Gabâ wants us to leave-a no trace dat we were 'ere, and no clues dat-a we are in any way connected to de... elimination of dose two. We are going to fill up de cellar wid-a liquid concrete and bury dem forever! Ha, ha, ha! I am-a so wicked!"

The other voices also laughed wickedly.

"But, boss, 'ow we gonna get the concrete into the cellar?"

"It's a good ting dat I am-a de one in charge, isn't it?" the voice of the boss said. "We canines can out-tink you 'umans every time! Dey are in a coal cellar, no? Dere is a trapdoor and a chute dat leads down from de street where-a de coal delivery used to be poured in. De chute is covered up by a piece of tin-a board in de cellar, but-a de weight of de concrete will break-a true, den de cellar will fill, and dey will be doomed! Ha, ha!" the voice chortled.

"Boss, how do you know that these instructions are really from the Great Gabâ and not from someone pretendin'?"

"Because, *stupido!*" the Italian voice said impatiently, "dey are using de secret sign at-a de end of de letter, de sign of-a de Tree Dog Biscuits. Dat proves it is a genuine instruction."

"Ha ha!" all the other voices said.

"When are we doing it, boss?" the first deep voice growled.

"In exactly tree hours, de concrete lorry will make-a its delivery. Dis gives-a me enough time to get a taxi to de airport. I can fly to 'ong Kong in-a time to meet one of de Great Gabâ's most trusted associates. And den I can-a tell him how marvellously efficient and evil we 'ave been! Ha ha!"

In the torchlight, Jeff and I looked at each other, first with shock and horror, but then both with a slow smile creeping into our expressions. We were both realising how we were going to escape.

Finding the thin board that blocked the old

coal chute wasn't difficult. Now that we knew it was there, simply knocking on the wall and listening to the different sounds the knocks made soon showed us where the board was. The hard, solid thud of the brick wall changed to a hollow, wooden sound, and showed us that the square board was on the wall, right in front of us. The reason that we couldn't see it was because of the darkness of the room, combined with the general dirtiness and dustiness of the walls. In the light of the phone torch, we could see that it was about the size of a small window.

Although finding the wooden board was easy, the next problem, the one of taking the board down, was rather difficult.

The board was attached to the wall at each corner by screws. They were screws that were driven in tightly and needed a screwdriver to remove them. We didn't have a screwdriver.

I sat down on the floor in the darkness and thought hard. There must be a solution. Jeff's only 'solution' was to shout in annoyance and stamp his foot in frustration.

"Gaaah!" he shouted. "So near yet so far!"

"Hang on, let me think," I replied.

I scratched at my collar with my hind foot, and in doing so the answer came to me.

"That's it!" I shouted. "My collar medallion!"

When I scratched, I had heard my metal collar medallion jangle in the quiet of the room. The medallion was bone-shaped and attached to the collar by a clip in the middle. My name and Jeff's mobile number were written on it, just in case something happened to me.

"Unclip my collar medallion," I ordered. "Use the end of the bone as a screwdriver. It's made of a very hard metal and should work perfectly."

"Brilliant!" Jeff exclaimed. "I'm on it."

I stood on my back legs with my front paw against him, so that he could easily reach my collar. Jeff quickly unclipped the medallion and examined the shape of the metal bone in the torchlight.

"It should fit perfectly," he declared, and he turned to the wall and started unscrewing the screws with our makeshift screwdriver. It took him quite a long time, as each screw was firmly screwed in. Whilst he worked, I stood still and thought.

I quickly came to a decision.

"Listen," I said, "as soon as we've escaped from this cellar, we need to jump in a taxi and go to your sister's house to get the money and passports."

"Oh?" he replied through clenched teeth, as he struggled with the screws. "Why is that? Do you fancy a nice relaxing beach holiday after this experience?"

"Well, not exactly a beach holiday, but a trip to Hong Kong instead. Ever been?" I asked.

"Of course not!" he replied, still unscrewing. "You know I've never really been anywhere."

"I think the man behind the newspaper would want us to go. If we've got to find out more about who's behind these chocolate robberies, then we've got to be at that meeting with Gabâ's trusted associate. In fact, we should try to be on the same flight as that boss dog who is meeting them."

Jeff stopped unscrewing for a moment. He looked at me in the light of the torch he held in his other hand.

"You're mad, but that's why I love you so much! What have we got to lose? After all, it's all paid for by MI5." He turned back to his unscrewing. "Nearly there," he puffed. "Ahh! There."

With the last screw no longer holding the board in place, it slid down to the floor of the cellar, settling with a clatter and a cloud of dust. Sunlight and sound flooded in and we both shielded our eyes, which had previously become adjusted to the dark.

We stood and looked up the chute to the street above. The hole was plenty big enough for us to be able to get up it. It sloped steeply up towards the outside world. At the top appeared to be an old iron grating that we could see people's feet walking over.

"There is nothing stopping me just pushing that grating up. It doesn't look like it's fixed at all," remarked Jeff. "I'll go up and push the grate and then I can lean down and pull you up."

"Great, go for it!" I said.

Jeff jumped up a little into the opening. At the same time, he pushed on both sides of the chute with his hands. He brought his knee up into the chute and was able to wedge himself. He reached up and pushed up against the grate. At first, it remained stuck and I felt a lurch in my tummy as I thought that our escape plan wasn't going to work. Suddenly the grate gave way with a clatter and flipped over onto the street above.

Jeff gripped the edge of the hole and pulled himself out. Then he lay down again on the pavement and reached down into the chute. I jumped up as high as I could, and grabbing hold of my front paws, Jeff was quickly able to help me up to street level. I shook myself whilst he carefully replaced the grate.

"Well, now we've gotta chute! Ha, chute, get it!" I said, pleased with my little 'chute', 'shoot' joke.

"That was rubbish," said Jeff. "Let's just get a taxi, quickly. We can pay the driver with some of the money left at Noola's house."

We soon hailed a black cab and it didn't take long to get back. The driver let me out to get some of the money that we had been given. Jeff unlocked the door and I went in, stood on my hind legs and grabbed some of the money from the table. I dashed back out to pay the driver, and then we both got safely into the house. For now at least, we could shut the yellow door on the danger that was outside. I wondered if our kidnap was covered by the 'Dangerous Dogs Act'.

CHAPTER 9
IN A JIFFY

"I need to sit down," Jeff said, flopping onto one of the soft chairs by the window. "That was terrifying."

"Oh yes," I agreed. "That was an unexpected adventure. I've never been kidnapped before! The man with the newspaper was right; we need to be careful from now on." I shook myself vigorously, as if to shake away all the danger that we had just experienced. "I'm just popping out of the back door for a wee." If you think I wee a lot, then you've never lived with a male dog.

In the yard, I looked around the top of the wall again for another imaginary finger. There was nothing to be seen, but I checked because places that were once safe felt like they could have hidden surprises.

Once back inside, with all the doors closed, I jumped up onto the other soft chair and curled up, ready for a much-needed power nap.

"Hmm, I'm not so sure that I want to do this anymore. It seems too dangerous," I heard Jeff murmur as I snuggled my head around near my tail.

Just then, we heard the key in the door and Noola walked in. As she stopped to hang her coat, she saw us and said, "Oh, you're already in. Did you have a nice time?"

"Erm…" Jeff replied. "Well, what happened was…"

"Phone Gizzmo," I said to my person. "Get her to book flights for us; we need to go to Hong Kong!"

"Why?" Noola asked from the kitchen, unpacking her shopping.

I quickly explained whilst she stood and looked shocked.

"Shouldn't you phone the police?" she asked, looking worried and wringing her hands.

"Normally, yes," I agreed, "but the man behind the newspaper said that this whole thing might become dangerous. Anyway, we haven't got time."

"But, just dashing off to Hong Kong? That's seems crazy!" Noola protested.

"Well, someone has just tried to murder us, so I'm feeling pretty crazy too," Jeff answered, waving his arms in the air as he spoke.

"We need to find out who's behind this," I said, stretching my front paws down onto the floor whilst leaving my back legs up on the chair for a moment.

"MI5 want us to find out what this is all about. Besides, isn't it going to be the most amazing adventure? Where is Hong Kong by the way?"

"Erm…" said Jeff. "I'll ask Gizzmo."

Jeff got through to Gizzmo, who was at home for once, sitting by her person's fire in their front room.

"I'm on it, dudes," she purred, when it had been explained to her what we wanted her to do. "I'll call you back with the flight information. Hong Kong, cool. That means going all the way to China! You want to go as soon as possible, right? Just give me all the new credit card details and I'll catch you later!"

"Well, you know where you are going now," Noola said. "You two had better start packing. It probably won't take Gizzmo long, if she's as good with computers as you say."

No sooner had Jeff and I managed to pack a few bare essentials, than Gizzmo video called us back again.

"Okay, dudes, I've sent all the details to your smartphone. You'd better call a taxi quick, as you need to be at Heathrow Airport really soon. A taxi is probably not the cheapest way, but you don't need to worry too much about cost anymore."

"Oh no!" Jeff shouted. "My phone was stolen by the kidnappers!"

At that moment, all of our heads turned at a tap on the window. There was no one there, but then the flap of the brass letter box opened, and a mysterious puffy brown jiffy bag was pushed through. It plopped down onto the door mat. I rushed over and picked it up in my mouth. I bounced back to my person and dropped it onto his lap. There was writing on the outside of the jiffy bag and he read it aloud: *You need to be much more careful.*

Jeff pulled open the bag and a phone dropped out. "It's my phone," he said. He pressed the 'on' button and there was a 'ping' as the information that Gizzmo had sent through appeared on the screen. "I wonder who on earth got my phone back for me," he pondered.

"Well, I think that MI5 are watching over us," I said. "Although how they managed to get it, I can't imagine."

"Worry about these things later, Ned," said Noola firmly. "Hurry, because you need to go."

It didn't take long for the taxi to come. As we needed to check in at the airport about two hours before our flight departed, we had only just enough time. We grabbed our passports, the credit card, the disguises and the money, then said our goodbyes. Jeff picked up our luggage and we jumped into the taxi. This was going to be a real-life, scary, exciting adventure!

CHAPTER 10
DINKY

In Bohol, life was taking a much more relaxed pace. The warmth of the sun soaked deeply into everything, from sea to tree, and from tourist to tarsier.

The little creatures lived in an area of the tropical forest not far from the famous Chocolate Hills. It was nearly the dry season in Bohol. The almost symmetrically-shaped, dome-like mounds of the Chocolate Hills were beginning to change to their famous chocolatey brown colour, giving them their name.

Tarsiers are mainly nocturnal, so during the daylight hours they don't move around much, but as the evening draws in, most of their food becomes active too.

"Dinky!" shouted Dinky's mum. "Dinky! I've just caught you a juicy beetle. Come here and eat it while it is fresh."

"Mum! I'm old enough to look after myself. Stop fussing," Dinky replied.

"Now look," said Dinky's mum, passing him the beetle that she clutched in her long fingers, "I want you to grow up to be a big, strong boy, and unless you eat properly, I'll always be worried about you."

There was not really much difference in size between Dinky and his mum. They were both small enough to easily fit into a human's palm, although it was their wonderfully large eyeballs, which weigh more than their brain, that was their main noticeable feature.

Dinky's mum made a grab at a passing butterfly and handed that to Dinky too.

"Now eat that as well, Dinky, just to please your mummy. Go on."

"Mum!" Dinky pleaded, whilst holding the now headless beetle in one hand. "Please stop calling me Dinky! It sounds so babyish. How is anyone going to take me seriously with a name like that! I've told you that I want to be called by my new name now. You know that it means 'divine retribution'. If I'm going to become a gangster gang leader, I've got to have a name that sounds a little mean."

"Well, you'll always be my little Dinky," said his mum. "And who are you really going to bring 'divine retribution' to, Dinky? I know we both feel really sad and angry about what happened to your father; he was such a good tarsier and I miss him terribly. But we're never going to be able to get our own back on the humans that did this. And if the only 'divine retribution' that you and your gang can dish out to the humans, is to try to let the tyres down of their Jeepneys… well, I don't really think that is going to bring the human race to its knees."

Dinky crunched on a spider that he'd just caught himself. He turned his head around completely to look behind him as he heard his smartphone vibrate. It was hidden in the fork of two tree branches so that his mum couldn't see it, but he had it on silent. He turned back to his mum.

"Look, Mum," he said, "it might not stop the humans, but at least I feel like we are doing something. And it's not *all* humans. I know there are some nice ones; they've built this tarsier sanctuary for us and they've now classed us an endangered species, to help try to protect us. But there are still some humans out there—."

"Yes, yes," interrupted Dinky's mum impatiently. "Whatever you get up to, just keep yourself safe. I'm off now to this spot I know, where the beetles are always big and easy to catch. Love you, Dinky!"

"Love you too, and stop calling me Dinky, remember it's… oh, never mind."

Dinky's mum had quickly moved out of sight, so he turned to look at the text message on his phone. It was from one of his gang members. They had just seen another group of tourists who would be just right for picking on. He knew that nothing was going to bring his father back, but when humans tried to take 'cute' tarsiers away from their native home and stick them in cages as pets... it made him feel so angry.

That's what had happened to his dad. His dad hadn't even survived long enough to leave the island. The stress of being caged had been too much for him, as it was for all tarsiers that had been kidnapped. He knew this because he'd overheard tourists talking. They said that the anguished tarsiers became so distressed that they bashed their little heads against the sides of the cages, killing themselves.

He had never told his mother this, as he knew that it would be too upsetting for her. This was the reason why he hated the humans so much. This was why he was going to take his revenge, to take divine retribution.

This was why he had become the Great Gabâ.

CHAPTER 11
CHOCCY YUM

At Heathrow Airport, Jeff and I checked in our baggage at the reception desk and went through airport security. I watched with amusement as Jeff was asked to remove his lace-up boots, his belt and other items of his clothing. Not for the first time, I thought how lucky I was not to have to be bothered with any of that. I was thoroughly sniffed by the security Springer Spaniel dogs, just to make sure I wasn't smuggling anything out of the country, but I don't mind being sniffed. It's good dog manners anyway.

In the large white and polished shopping area, we followed the path of carpet that led us through all the different products on sale.

"What have you got there?" I asked, looking up at my person as he struggled with armfuls of chocolate bars.

"This chocolate is so cheap!" he exclaimed. "I know that you can't eat it, Ned, but I love chocolate and I've never seen it so cheap; it's less than half the price it normally is." He tried to pile even more onto his already precariously loaded arms, tucking some under his chin to help hold the pile steady.

"It's another sign of global warming, you know," I said. "Gizzmo was telling me about it. Chocolate is getting more expensive to produce. Climate change has affected how the cocoa crop has grown this year."

"Oh yeah?" mumbled my person, from underneath an ever-increasing pile of chocolate bars.

"All chocolate is made from the cocoa plant," I continued. "So if the crop fails then it's going to be harder to produce chocolate."

"Well, how come this stuff is so cheap then?" came the muffled reply.

I looked at one of the wrappers of a bar that had fallen to the floor.

"Because," I replied, "that stuff is not actually chocolate. It's a chocolate-flavoured candy snack," I read from the wrapper. "It says, *Choccy Yum, the chocolatiest chocolate-flavoured tasting snack. It's all flavouring and sugar.*"

Crash! Jeff dropped the huge pile of Choccy Yum bars onto the floor. "I don't want that! That sounds gross!"

"A wise decision," I agreed. "But we'd better move quickly and hide because I don't think that the airport security people are going to be very pleased with all the Choccy Yum bars that you have just dropped over the floor."

"Those Choccy Yum people are cheats," Jeff complained. "Pretending their bars are chocolate, when they are nothing but a cheap imitation."

"Cheats they may be," I said, weaving around the stands of magazines to try and avoid detection by the gathering store detectives. "But their deception works, because you were about to buy them!"

We walked away quickly, trying not to look suspicious, stopping occasionally to pretend to be interested in a certain perfume or a particular snazzy-looking watch. I paused for a minute by one of the animal gadget stands; the automatic food packet opener looked good.

We approached the people's toilets and the specially designated area of animal toileting. It was an AstroTurf space, enclosed behind a glass window. The special attendant was on hand to ensure that the animals' people picked up their poos. As the glass door opened to let a happy tan-coloured Pug out, I caught the wonderful smell of other dogs' wee in my nostrils. It brought on that feeling that I had to go too.

"I'm just going to the dog loo before we board!" I called.

"I'll go too," Jeff replied. "Just keep an eye out, though; we don't want to be snatched again, but we do want to see if you can listen out for the kidnappers' leader. He'll be around somewhere, probably getting the same flight."

"Yes, he did have a very distinctive Italian voice. I would definitely recognise it if I heard it again. I'm not sure if it was male or female, though. It could have been either."

"Just listen out," Jeff said. "We should have put our disguises on before we left, but I didn't think. I've packed them both in our suitcases."

Jeff disappeared into the gents and I went into the dog toilet room. The attendant gave me a few disapproving looks for coming in with no human to accompany me, but I waited around and just had a few wees until I could see my person outside, looking through the glass. I indicated to him that he needed to come in. He pulled a dog poo bag out of his pocket and he stood ready to pick up my poo. He tied up the bag and threw it into the dog poo bin by the door. As we both stepped outside, back onto the white tiles of the concourse, Jeff looked up at the flight departures board and saw that our boarding gate was open. We needed to make our way to the departure lounge.

This was the dangerous bit, because if the boss with the Italian accent was getting the same flight as us, here was the place where we might bump into each other. We were not sure what he or she looked like. Neither of us spoke, because we wanted to listen out for that voice.

It was hard to not talk, though, when came to the travelators. They were such fun! As

I hopped onto the moving walkway, the ground moved beneath my feet. Jeff and I were whisked along in the direction of the departure gate. Jeff could hold onto the moving hand rail for balance, but although I had four feet keeping me steady, I couldn't help almost tripping as the travelator came to the end and deposited us back onto the tiled floor. We looked at each other and grinned. Airports were such fun!

I felt guilty for enjoying myself when I remembered that we could so easily have been seen by the criminals as we whizzed along. Perhaps we were. Jeff swallowed hard when I reminded him.

Whilst we waited in the final queue, to show our boarding passes before we boarded the aeroplane, Jeff's phone rang. It was Gizzmo.

"Yo, dudes! You guys have just gotta check out the news! This is just taking it to a whole new level! Check it out!" She rang off.

"What is it?" I asked. "What on the news?"

"I'm not sure," Jeff answered, "but just wait a minute, we are about to board. We'll be able to see the news on the in-flight screens when we get on. We've got business class tickets too! That means that we have got nice seats. Exciting!"

We carried on moving along with the rest of the travellers who were flying with us.

"Gizzmo booked the tickets for us," said Jeff. "She said that we are on business. Her Majesty's Secret Service business!"

We walked with the other passengers through the tunnel that led to the door of the aircraft. I was eager to see what Gizzmo was so urgently contacting us about. What could have happened now?

CHAPTER 12
THE VOICE

I
t was a large aircraft, so there were three sections of seats with two corridors that ran the length of the cabin area. We had our own individual sections that were partitioned off. This gave even tall humans enough leg room to stretch out and sleep, and we animals could curl up easily. In the middle of the three seating sections, Jeff and I both had a corridor to the sides of us.

"Quick, let's get the news on," said Jeff. "We can see what Gizzmo was talking about."

I managed to press on a button and the news flashed up on a small screen. Jeff switched his on too. There was the usual moving strapline at the bottom of the screen, but I couldn't hear anything.

"You'll need these... er, sir," the passing flight

attendant correctly guessed, as she leaned over me and passed me a set of headphones.

Her red and blue uniform and little hat made her look very smart, and I felt very glamorous travelling on an aeroplane. She passed me a little zip-up bag that contained a small chew for fresh breath and a few other useful items, like nose balm. This helped with the dry air from the air conditioning.

She helped me on with my headphones and asked, "Would you like a drink, sir?"

Before she could tell me a list of options, I said, "Flat Bright, please!"

Jeff leaned over the partition and said to me, "Hey, Ned! Not too many of those. I don't want to spend the flight getting up and taking you to the toilet every two minutes. Now, have you managed to hear the news headlines yet?"

"No, not yet," I answered.

"Well, apparently…" He paused whilst the flight attendant returned with our drinks. "You know the big chain of famous chocolate shops in most high streets in the country? There are two big ones: 'Zorntons' and 'The Premier Choc'. Well, they've nearly all been raided, simultaneously!"

"No!" I exclaimed. "All at the same time? When? How?"

"The news is just in," he replied, leaning over the partition and waving his champagne glass around as he talked. "They aren't sure of all the details yet; it's only just happened. Just as the shops were closing, before any of them might have pulled down their metal shutters, the dogs struck! It happened all across the UK. It appears that the nationwide spate of mobility scooter thefts was no coincidence. The gangs of dogs that stole them were preparing their fleet of 'attack vehicles'. CCTV footage shows the dogs coming together at pre-planned spots. They were riding the mobility vehicles into the chocolate shop windows." He took another sip of the delicious Champagne and I waited for him to go on.

"The rest of the gang of dogs came in behind them and ate or just chomped up as much chocolate as possible. The dogs just ran away after that, splitting up and disappearing down alleyways into the night."

"That's incredible!" I exclaimed. "It's almost as if the first lot of attacks were like little practice runs for this big attack. Do you know what else has been said about it?"

We had to wait because a voice over the loudspeakers said that we needed to turn off our phones, we should fasten our seatbelts, secure all luggage in overhead lockers and prepare for take-off.

"If you look up at your screen now, Ned, you can see the Prime Minister talking. She has said that she condemns these cowardly attacks in the strongest terms and that the security services are on a very high level of alert—"

"Oh look!" I interrupted, pointing to the screen. "There's Larry, the cat who is in charge at Number Ten Downing Street."

"Oh yes! It must be important. But an expert has already said that this has caused a chocolate supply crisis across our country. The price of chocolate will definitely go up. It will be so expensive that only the rich will be able to afford it—"

"Oh, they are going to show us the safety checks and prepare for take-off," I interrupted again, wiggling myself firmly back into my seat. "I'm sure chocolate prices will soon get back to normal again. By the way, what's flying like? Will I enjoy it?" I asked.

"I've been told it's great fun. I think you'll love it," Jeff replied. "Yes, chocolate prices will return to normal, but it'll take a while until enough cocoa can be imported for the chocolate factories to restore supplies. They will have to replace all the chocolate that's been scoffed by the dog gangs. I wish I'd bought all of that cheap Choccy Yum stuff we saw in the airport shop."

"Choccy Yum? No, you don't!" I warned. "That wasn't even real chocolate; that stuff was a cheat. I bet a lot of people will be buying it, though, if chocolate becomes as expensive as you say. Anyway, they wouldn't have let you bring all that onto the plane. Your big armfuls far exceeded your baggage allowance."

Our aircraft started taxiing along on our short journey to where we were going to take off. Once the aeroplane was in position, I heard the engines start to quietly rev up and our speed began to increase for take-off.

I was able to see the airport go flashing by through the small window in the side of the plane and felt the acceleration push me back into my seat. It was very exciting and I felt a little disappointed that it was all over so quickly. We began to level out; the flight attendants unclipped their seatbelts and started walking about the cabin. The *undo seatbelt* sign pinged on and I pulled the animal release cord with my teeth, to unclip mine.

"Did you enjoy the take-off?" Jeff asked.

"Oh yes! It was great! How about you?"

"Yes, I enjoyed it. I've heard landing can be good fun too, but in a different way. You'll definitely like this next bit," he said. "They will be offering you food! Now have a look at the menu. Gizzmo said in her travel details email that she'd ordered you a special doggy menu. What's the matter, Ned? You're looking a bit fidgety."

"Sorry, I may have had a few too many Flat Brights. Would you take me to the toilet, please?"

"Sure, Ned. I'm also thinking that after we've had some food, we'll need some sleep. Fourteen hours is going to be a long flight!"

Jeff walked around to my seat and I jumped down. I followed him along the cabin to the toilet signs. The light above the toilet door showed that no one was in there, so my person opened the door to a small room like a cupboard, where the human toilet was. He closed the door behind us and reached down to the metal handle on the floor marked *Animal toilet*.

He turned the handle and a large hatch in the floor opened on metal levers. It revealed an area of flat sand, like a small sand pit.

"Thank goodness," I said. "I'm dying to go!"

I went for a wee on the sand and stepped back onto the metal aeroplane floor. Jeff closed the trapdoor and pressed the flush. We smelled the strong antiseptic smell as a spray shot out underneath the trapdoor, over the sand.

"What would happen if I wanted a poo?" I asked.

"We'd use a dog poo bag like we normally do." He read the sign and tapped a dispenser on the wall. "And then post it down this chute here," he said, pointing to another little trapdoor halfway up the wall.

"Ah, very clever," I remarked. I stood aside as he unlocked the toilet door and walked forward, back into the main cabin again.

"Stop!" I hissed. "Close the door again, but leave it open a crack and listen. Does that voice sound familiar to you?"

We stood still and listened again. That voice was unmistakable.

Suddenly a shadow appeared at the crack in the door. I ducked as a hand shot through the crack above me and pulled the door open.

"Are you all right there, sir? Can I give you any assistance? Is the door stuck?"

I looked up at the hand and the painted fingernails, and then across to the smiling face of one of the cabin crew. "Erm, thanks, no… we're fine," I mumbled.

"Yes. Thanks," Jeff agreed.

We walked slowly out from the toilet. Neither of us wanted to walk too far away as we tried to hear the voice again. Unfortunately, the flight attendant also stood waiting.

"Can I help you back to your seats?" she politely asked.

"No, we're fine, thanks. We're just stretching our legs," Jeff replied cheerfully. There was nothing else for it but to make our way back to our seats without drawing any further attention to ourselves. I jumped up onto my seat and Jeff went around to his. When he got there, we both leaned over the partition again to talk in hushed tones.

"That voice, did you hear it?" I asked.

"What, the voice that sounded exactly like the one you heard in the coal cellar in Brick Lane? The voice of the boss? The reason that we are flying off to Hong Kong to try and be at the meeting?"

"Yes, that voice. I'm one hundred percent sure that was the same voice. We didn't see the owner of the voice in London, so this is our chance to find out who it belongs to!" I said excitedly.

"Okay," Jeff said, trying to stay calm. "You have the best hearing and you are the least likely to be noticed, so I think you should slowly make your way down the aisle again and see if you can get a glimpse of the speaker."

"Agreed," I said. "I've just got to try and avoid the flight attendant; otherwise, she might draw everyone's attention by speaking to me."

"Well, as there are two aisles," Jeff suggested, "all you have to do is wait until she walks down one side and then you go up the other side. As you are not very tall, she won't see you over the seats."

"She's coming down the aisle on my side now," I whispered excitedly. "There's no time like the present."

With that, I hopped down to the floor and made my way around the end of the seating section. I then casually wandered up the other aisle, passing my person and towards where we had heard the voice. I sauntered as slowly as I could, without wanting to look too strange, listening all the time.

Moving slowly gave me a chance to properly look at some of the other passengers. There were a few sleeping humans who had already stretched out and covered themselves with blankets.

There was a rich-looking white Siamese cat, with a diamond collar that glinted in the cabin lights. She was curled up in her seat and was purring gently as she slept. There were humans of all ages with their headphones on, staring at the in-flight movie screens in front of them. I passed a Golden Retriever, nodding his headphone-wearing head, up and down in time to the music he was listening to.

I sauntered past an Italian Greyhound, with a flashy gold chain around his neck. He had his nose up against the television in front of him, like I do when I'm reading the small writing along the bottom of the screen. I walked on past him and was nearly at the end of the seating section again, near to where the toilets were. I knew I had better keep an eye out for the flight attendant making her way back again.

Then I heard it again. The voice.

I whipped my head around to glance backwards once more. It was coming from the Italian Greyhound watching the news, speaking in an Italian accent. He was commenting on it to whoever was across the aisle from him. I knew straight away which news article they were watching.

"Ha ha!" he chuckled. "Dey've-a really done it now! Wid all dat-a proper chocolate gone, all de chocoholics in de UK will-a have to buy our cheap rubbish. *Fantastico*!" He flung his front paws around in little circles as he spoke.

I lurked just on the corner of the seats, keeping an eye out for an approaching flight attendant.

"Yeah!" growled a deep cockney voice in reply, which I had also heard from the coal cellar. "Gabâ's plan worked then. But I don't understand 'ow it's going t'make us rich, boss? 'specially since the fake chocolate is so cheap."

"Make-a *us* rich, you say?" said the Italian Greyhound. "Since when were you a boss in dis enterprise? Eh? Well, let-a me tell you dat Choccy Yum isn't always going to be cheap. *Si*, yes, it's extremely cheap to make, because all it is made from, is a few chemicals. It's barf-room cleaning powder, flavouring and a few everyday tings-a like dat. When we have stopped de supply of proper cocoa pods, dey can't make any *bene*, er… good chocolate in the UK.

We'll put-a de price up den! By dat time, people will be super desperate and dey will-a buy any-ting, even Choccy Yum. Ha ha!"

"What, you mean that when something is 'arder t'get 'old of, it becomes more expensive? So if it's easy t'get 'old of, then it's cheaper t'buy. Well, that makes sense. Why just in the UK though, boss? Don't uver people eat chocolate too?"

"Of course-a dey do," the Italian Greyhound said. "But de UK is de world's largest consumer of chocolate, so it's a great-a place to start. Dat's why we are meeting one of de Great Gabâ's representatives in 'ong Kong, so we can make-a plans to spread de idea worldwide. We'll 'ave great news of our success to tell dem. What better place to meet dem dan on top of de world, in de 'ighest bar in de world? Ha ha! We are meeting in time to watch de sun go down. It will be going down-a on de world of proper chocolate companies."

"In time t'watch the sun go down? Wot ya mean, boss?"

"It's a little joke, Boris. My goodness, you just can't get-a de staff nowadays. It's a double meaning: 'de sun go down' as in meeting at sunset and 'de sun go down', meaning de end of some-ting. Now-a I'm going to sleep. I suggest you do de same."

Just then, the flight attendant came around the corner.

"Hello again, sir," she said to me. "Can I be of some assistance?"

I tried to move on so as not to be seen if anyone looked up. I heard a rustle as Boris looked around. I dashed past the flight attendant and back down the other aisle, towards my seat.

I heard Boris ask the flight attendant, "'Oo was that then, just standing there?"

"No one, sir, just another passenger. Can I be of any assistance to you?"

Back in my seat, I told Jeff what I had discovered.

"That is fantastic work, Ned! You'll make an excellent spy; MI5 will be very pleased with you. I can't wait till we land so that we can tell Gizzmo. Now I wonder where the highest bar in the world is. I vaguely remember reading about it in one of the newspapers. Never mind, we can ask Gizzmo to find out for us when we speak to her. We really need sleep. Try to get some. Goodnight."

I tried to sleep but felt too nervous with the criminals so close. So there was quite a lot of movie-watching and a large amount of eating. There were also a couple more toilet breaks, in which Jeff managed to walk past the Italian Greyhound and get a look himself.

He saw that Boris was a mixed breed of dog. He was quite large and scruffy, with dark brown and black fur, and sharp-looking teeth. Jeff managed to take a photo with his phone camera whilst they both slept. MI5 would be proud of him too. That was something else we could ask Gizzmo to find out about. Who were they?

I looked out of the window as we approached Hong Kong and saw the lovely blue sea and the tall, closely packed buildings of the city, with hills behind them.

The aeroplane slowly banked over to the side and the view out of the window changed from the coastline to a view of the clear blue sky. We levelled out again and I heard the engine noise change. There was a funny feeling in my tummy as the plane slowly dropped in altitude towards the runway.

We arrived at about seven o'clock in the morning in Hong Kong time. My person was right about landing. That was one of the fun bits too! The pilot was skilful and we touched down very gently. I felt myself being pressed against my seatbelt a little as we decelerated quickly and slowed down to a stop.

"Duck down and look busy when the criminals come past us," Jeff warned me. "Let's let them go first, as it will be much better to have them in front of us where we can see them."

"Good idea," I replied. "I'll rummage around under my seat until they have gone."

When it was safe for us to go, we got up, and Jeff grabbed his bag. The flight attendant stood beside the door and just behind her stood the captain of the aeroplane. The captain was a classy-looking Afghan Hound, her long hair groomed to perfection. She was wearing her cap leaning at a jaunty angle, her collar glittering with the golden wings that showed her rank. She watched her passengers disembark with a nod and a smile. We said our thank-yous as we passed them.

"You're welcome!" said the flight attendant. "I hope you had a pleasant flight. Thank you for flying with us today."

I smiled to myself as I thought about the idea of a 'pleasant flight' with the criminals on board. I scurried quickly along the tunnel and then we followed the signs to passport control. The customs officers gave our passports a quick check, making sure our photos matched how we looked, then handed them back. Off we went to reclaim our baggage. All the time we had to take extra care not to be seen by the two chocolate cheats!

Gizzmo had sent us clear instructions about what to do when we left the airport. Close to the baggage reclaim carousel was a train station. Here, we could take the MTR, the Hong Kong version of the London tube train. The bags with wheels rolled easily straight onto the waiting train carriage, which was spacious and travelled smoothly. Gizzmo had told us to take the train right into Hong Kong Island and then to take a taxi to our hotel. She had also booked the hotel for us online.

We jumped into a waiting taxi and, as we did not speak Chinese, Jeff showed the driver the address of the hotel on his phone. The driver nodded and said, "Yes," to show that he knew where the place was.

Whilst we travelled, Jeff and I chatted about the different smells, the busy roads and traffic, and the amazing tall, new buildings next to little narrow streets, as we got near to our hotel. Most buildings had big grey air conditioning units bolted high up on the outside. These were mixed with old-style rickety wooden buildings. Some were open-fronted, with no windows at all.

I couldn't help thinking about how this was a different country with different smells, different dogs, different food and different customs. It was wonderful to be here, but if something bad were to happen to us, who would come to our rescue?

CHAPTER 13
THE VIEW FROM HERE

I t felt very warm and at last, in the hotel room, we
could relax for a moment and sit and stop travelling,
enjoying the cool air conditioning.

"Ah well," Jeff said, "we've got a few hours until
sunset, so we'd better get in contact with Gizzmo, and
find out what we are up against!"

"If you video call her now," I asked, "what time
will it be in England?"

"Good point, Ned," Jeff replied. "Let's find out
first."

He logged into the hotel's Wi-Fi, using the code
that the cat on the reception desk had given us. He
asked the phone's built-in voice-activated software to
answer the question: "What time is it in the UK when
it is nine o'clock in the morning in Hong Kong?"

The phone didn't really understand the question.

"Just type it into the search engine instead," I suggested.

"All right, the answer is that it is one in the morning in the UK. It's the middle of the night," Jeff said forlornly.

"That's all right then," I said, feeling pleased. "Don't forget, Gizzmo is a cat. Cats are always out doing things at night. I think they are pretty nocturnal, although Gizzmo is quite lazy; I don't think she'll be out prowling around the streets. Give her a call."

"Of course. I'll do it now then, and I'll send her the pictures I've taken. Let's see if she can find out who they are. If not, then I'm sure the man behind the newspaper will know."

"Hey, dudes!" answered Gizzmo when Jeff called. You could see from her surroundings that she was in the same place that she was when we last talked to her. She was in her front room next to the fire, although this time it was dark, as her person had gone to bed. Cats don't really need the light on to see in the dark. I could, however, see the blue glow of a television coming from the far corner of the room, and wondered what Gizzmo could be watching at this time of night.

"The dude behind the newspaper from MI5 told me that you had landed safely. I guess you saw the news. You were right about the organised crime thing. How did those dudes pull that one off?"

"It was quite an amazing crime," I agreed. "Our news is that, while we were on the plane, we came across the criminals who kidnapped us and who are having the meeting in Hong Kong. It's the meeting that we need to listen in on. But hey, we've taken photos of them and we can send the pictures to you and the man behind the newspaper. What we need you to do now, though, is find the answer to these questions: they are going to have their meeting in the highest bar in the world, when the sun goes down. So *where* is this, and *when* is this?"

"No worries, dudes. I'll find these things out straight away and get right back to you. By the way, how's the hotel room? I had to book it in a hurry and did not have much time to check if it was a cool one."

"It's just fine, thanks. We might only be sleeping in it for a night. I'm going to send those photos off now. Something tells me that MI5 will be awake too. What are you watching on the TV by the way?"

"Erm… hey, dude. It's just something that I like to do now and then, ya know?"

She looked away from the camera; I'd never seen Gizzmo look embarrassed before. "It's just KVC," she went on. "You know, dude, Kat Value Convenience, the cats' shopping channel. I just love ordering new stuff, it's really cool. I've ordered a great new scratching post. It's got these way cool dangly things on."

"Gizzmo!" I exclaimed, "How many scratching posts do you need? You have eleven different ones already; your person told Jeff that most of them aren't even taken out of their wrapping."

"Dude!" replied Gizzmo. "You just can't have enough scratching posts, y'know? You never know when you might get the urge to dig those claws into something."

I left Gizzmo to her research and turned my attention back to our current situation.

Jeff got the spy phone out, the one that the man behind the newspaper had given him. "I used this one to take the photographs," he said. "It's got a really good camera."

We looked at the photos of the two criminals. They were very clear. It showed the Italian Greyhound and Boris, his big, hairy companion, fast asleep in their seats.

"I'll ask the question, *Who are these two and is there anything we should know?* and text that with the photos," Jeff said. He pressed the send button.

We explored the hotel room whilst we waited, and looked at the amazing view out of the window. I didn't realise quite how high up we were. The windows went from floor to ceiling and around the corner. It gave us views of all the other impressively tall buildings, built very close together. By standing next to the window and looking as far as I could around the corner, I could see the glistening blue water of Hong Kong Harbour. There were a few boats making their way slowly up and down the waterway.

Jeff made himself a coffee from the machine in the little kitchen.

"Is there any…?" I started to say.

"Yes, I've made you a Flat Bright too," he laughed. "I'll put it over here for you."

"Aww, thanks!" I said. "Oh, I can hear a buzzing. Is that from one of your phones that's on silent?"

"Yes, it is, you're right!" he replied, grabbing the spy phone from the tabletop. "It's from the man behind the newspaper, or at least from MI5. It's a text that says… oh dear, that doesn't sound good… it says, *Well done for making contact with the targets. One is Boris 'Chunky' Chuggworth, a well-known criminal and wanted London thug. The other… the Italian Greyhound… is Carlos Fandango, also wanted by Interpol… the international police. Both dogs are extremely dangerous and should not be approached. Be very careful.*"

"Oh, well, that's going to be tricky," I said. "We're supposed to be following them."

"Yes, but where?" wondered Jeff. "I hope Gizzmo gets back to us soon. We've got to be at that meeting today. It's our only chance to find out who's behind all this."

I went back to looking out of the window. Jeff made himself another coffee and then sat down again, tapping his foot as he waited. I used the indoor dog toilet facilities.

Jeff's own phone rang with the sound that announced a video call. I jumped onto the seat next to him as he held his phone up so that I could see Gizzmo. She was still there in front of the fire.

"Yo, dudes, here we go! This is what you wanna know!" she chanted in a rap as she spoke. Gizzmo peered at her laptop. "The highest bar in the world is called Ozone. It's at the top of the fifth highest building in the world, which is the Ritz-Carlton building, just across the harbour from you, in Kowloon. The sun sets tonight at half-past six, so if I were you I would start making your way there now."

"Okay, good work, Gizzmo," I said. "How do we get there?"

"Dude, you are now on Hong Kong Island, so if you get the Poodle Maps up on your phone, you can make your way down to Victoria Harbour. Get the Star ferry across to the Kowloon side. Once you are there, just get a taxi. You dudes want to be there in plenty of time so that you can get a look around the bar, and look at the amazing view. It's one hundred and eighteen floors up! You'll need to find a good place to sit."

"That's very sensible; we don't want to be seen," Jeff agreed.

"Is it going to be time for the disguises?" I suggested. "That's just the sort of occasion that they might come in useful."

"Okay, dudes, do what you need to do to stay safe. Good luck!" called Gizzmo, and closed the connection.

I jumped down from the chair and looked at my reflection in the hotel room mirror, imagining myself a different colour and with a large moustache.

"Mmm…" mused Jeff, looking at me and stroking his chin in thought. "Yes, I think this might just be the time for you to become Nedmondo. Here's the stuff that you need – give me a shout if you want help applying your hair dye. I'm going to try out these MI5 contact lenses."

A few minutes later, we had become our new selves, so to speak.

"John Smith," I remarked, looking at my squinting and blinking person. He was getting used to wearing his contact lenses instead of his glasses. His stick-on bushy moustache kept on wiggling from side to side as he screwed his face up. "You are going to have to try to relax when you wear your disguise," I said. "You'll draw attention to yourself with all those weird faces you are making."

"It's all right for you, Nedmondo, with your cool name and your dashing moustache. Even your golden hair colour makes you look suave and interesting."

"I don't know about that," I replied. "But I very much doubt that we would be recognised now. Let's just go, and try to remember that there are lots of people relying on us to solve this mystery."

We did not have much else to get ready because we hadn't really unpacked. Jeff clipped my lead on, and it didn't take us long to be out of the hotel and start making our way down to the harbour, following the map on the phone.

The streets were busy with people and traffic. Everyone was very friendly, and if we took a wrong turn we just asked a dog, cat or human. We could make ourselves understood by using signs and pointing, so we were quickly put on the right track again.

It was very hot and I was glad that Jeff had brought a bottle of water with him. When we got to the busy pier beside the harbour, we both paused to have another drink. Jeff poured me some into our fold-up travel water bowl.

With our tickets, we only needed to wait a few minutes before the old green and white ferry chugged its way to the pier. As we got on board, we heard two English tourists saying that there had been a ferry here since 1888. Gizzmo could have told us other ways to get to Kowloon, through tunnels or over bridges, but this way gave us some great views of Hong Kong. The amazing tall buildings along the waterside, with a backdrop of mountains and blue sky, were certainly very impressive. It was reassuring to smell salty sea air again.

Once disembarked, we had no problem in quickly getting a taxi from the taxi rank. I climbed in and only had to say 'Ritz-Carlton' to the driver for us to be once again joining the busy, beeping traffic.

I hopped down onto the pavement when the driver stopped. I had a sniff of an often-used wee spot and added to it myself. Jeff paid the driver and joined me at the bottom of the front steps. We looked around nervously, both at the impressive and grand front of the tall building, and up and down the pavement, in case the criminals were already here. This whole thing, which had seemed a bit of an exciting adventure a few hours ago, all now seemed very real and dangerous.

"Here we go," said Jeff. I had one final shake and followed him closely as he went up the steps, into the luxuriously decorated reception area.

We didn't speak to each other but walked quickly across the shiny marble floor, following the signs to the lifts. Inside, there was a big mirror in which we saw our reflections. As the doors closed behind us, Jeff stared up at the amazing choice of floors on the lift buttons. There was a similar set of animal 'nose' buttons nearer to the floor so that we could reach.

"Which one?" he asked, turning his head to look down at me.

"The highest one, of course!" I answered.

"But Gizzmo said it was on the hundred and eighteenth floor. These buttons don't go that high."

"Just choose the highest number and we'll see what to do after that," I suggested.

As he pressed the button, we started to feel the lift moving, very smoothly, but in a way that felt we were moving up very fast.

"What if it stops and criminals get into our lift?" I asked.

"Then we're doomed!" he answered darkly. My person looked at me and smiled a little nervously.

"Don't worry," he said. "Let's just hope our luck holds out."

After what seemed like no time at all, the lift stopped and the doors opened onto another reception area. I saw a smart-looking Boston Terrier talking in a quite haughty tone to a member of the hotel staff. You could tell by the staff's body language that the Boston Terrier was a very important visitor.

I looked around for a sign to give us a clue as to where we should go next. Across the reception area were directions for visitors to other things that could be found on this floor. There were beauty salons and very expensive jewellery shops, but at the very end of the list was a smaller plaque saying *Ozone – up*!

"Over here," I said, leading the way into the lift. We got in and once again pressed the highest number button. This lift was smaller and moved faster. I really felt like I was going up at speed. There was a funny feeling in my tummy, the sort of feeling you get when you go quickly over a humpbacked bridge in a car. Then we stopped. The door opened and we were there. This was the place where we would find out the answers to all our questions.

CHAPTER 14
MI5 ARE LISTENING

The lift doors opened to reveal another reception area. This one was smaller with dim lighting, but not in any way less grand. The floor, unlike the rest of the building, was of shiny black marble, and tiled using tessellating irregular pentagons. The walls were lined with a golden network of irregular tessellating shapes, inlayed into the walls. The ceiling too, I noticed, was decorated with a similar style. It gave the impression of being inside an ice cave.

In front of us, just before you entered the bar itself, was a small desk.

"Hello and welcome to Ozone," said a smartly dressed receptionist. On the desk in front of her sat a black miniature Schnauzer. He tried to smile, showing his front teeth in rather an unnerving way. I knew the feeling. Dogs can't really smile like humans.

Just at that very moment, there came a buzz from Jeff's pocket.

"It's the… you know… other phone!" I tried to say without sounding suspicious. "You had better see what it says. It could be important."

"Yes," Jeff agreed. "Excuse me a minute!" he said to the receptionists.

He took a step back from the desk and pulled out the device. "It's a text, look." He turned the spy phone towards me and I saw that the text said: *I'm going to ring you in thirty seconds. Make sure you cannot be overheard.*

We both stepped away from the reception desk and stood together. Jeff shuffled beside and then behind a tall plant pot. It smelt very dusty and the crumbs on the floor showed that someone had been secretly munching biscuits here.

The phone, which was on silent, rang its rhythmic buzz. Jeff crouched down to me and tried to make sure that I could hear too.

"Hello, gentlemen," the voice said, which I instantly recognised as that of the man behind the newspaper. "We have been tracking you closely and we know that you are about to enter the meeting place. You must not be seen by anyone at the meeting. Have you brought your disguises? Good fellows. Be careful that the glue holding the moustaches on doesn't come loose in the heat. You must get as close as you can without raising any suspicions. We wish you to try and record the conversations you hear, because we need these as evidence later. On your phone is an app called *MI5 Can Hear You*. Activate the app, and leave the phone turned on in your pocket when the meeting begins. We will be able to hear everything. I do mean everything, so be careful when you go to the toilet. That is all, good luck. Oh, enjoy the light show if you are still there at eight o'clock. It's rather good."

The man behind the newspaper cut the connection and Jeff activated the app called *MI5 Can Hear You*. The 'on' function was a big red button in the centre of the screen. "I'll turn it on when the meeting starts," he said.

"Right, well, let's go in!" I said, pretending to be cheerful, in a way I didn't feel.

We walked towards the receptionists again. They both 'smiled' at us and the lady indicated with her arm gesture for us to walk into the bar.

The inside was decorated in the same way as the reception area, but even more so. It really did feel as if you were inside a giant ice cube or cave. Maybe this was what it felt like to be in a cloud. The low purple lighting and the icicle-like hangings all contributed to this effect. But it was the windows on the wall opposite that gave the most amazing thing of all. From the one hundred and eighteenth floor, they gave a breathtaking view over Victoria Harbour and the tall, glass, modern skyscrapers of Hong Kong. The light was beginning to fade outside as sunset approached. The illuminations were just becoming visible.

"Wow! That is some view!" I exclaimed. "We are so high up, it's like looking from the windows of an aeroplane."

"No wonder we felt funny coming up in the lift," Jeff said. "Come on, let's look outside on the outdoor terrace and then we should get a drink. We need to blend in."

We looked out over the edge of the building at the little boats that were travelling up and down and across the waterway. We were so high up that my brain was unable to understand what it was seeing. This meant that I didn't feel at all frightened by the drop beneath me, just fascinated by what I could see.

"Flat Bright?" Jeff asked me as we approached the bar.

"Erm, have they got anything else? Like meat-infused water perhaps? With ice, please, I'm feeling posh," I answered, looking around for a seat. "I'll go and sit over here. This way, we can see the door when they come in, but that pillar will hide us."

"Okay, see you there," replied Jeff, as he waited for the drinks to be poured.

I jumped up onto the seat and waited for him to come over.

"This is a good spot that you chose," Jeff said, putting our drinks down on the table, mine in a wide silver dish so that I could easily lap at it.

"They will be here in a minute. Gizzmo said sunset was at half-past six."

The bar wasn't crowded but there were a variety of different customers. Most were tourists, who had come up for the awe-inspiring experience. There was a Red Setter, clearly exhausted by the whole thing, curled up and asleep in a chair. His people – a man, a lady and three children – sipped drinks and shared a bowl of coloured ice cream scoops.

The Red Setter woke up at the clink of spoons against the bowl, as indeed would I!

When the group of criminals came into the bar, and wonderfully took the seats that were just on the other side of the pillar, we hardly noticed them. They all looked so ordinary. A large man in a suit and dark glasses, with a fierce black Doberman Pinscher, entered first. *They are here for security*, I thought. Next came a bald businessman in a light blue suit. He accompanied a smart, pretty lady dog, a white fluffy Bichon Frise. They were all respectably dressed and groomed, talking politely. They sat down at their table. Had it not been for the Italian Greyhound and the big hairy dog with him, we would not have thought anything was suspicious.

Jeff casually took his spy phone out and pressed the red 'go' button to start recording. I knew that I needed to look relaxed and not nervous, but I felt that I wanted to just run away. I realised again that I couldn't just run home, even if I had the chance.

The criminal gathering all sat around a marble-topped table. The dogs were sitting up on the chairs with their front legs straight in front of them, and the humans were confidently lounging back, all facing each other.

"Well," said the high Italian-voiced Carlos Fandango, having lapped from his silver bowl in front of him. "I'll-a start wid de talk, as dey say. Ha ha! Why 'ave you called dis-a meeting, and when are you going to pay us for our successful job?" He directed this to the lady Bichon Frise.

"Not so fast," she said slowly and calmly, raising her paw as a signal to stop. "That's not how we do business around here. We like to have certain polite pleasantries and chat first. It keeps everything civilised."

"Oh-a no," continued the Italian Greyhound. "I did not-a fly 'alfway around de world to waste time on pleasantries. Let's-a get on wid it."

The smartly dressed businessman who accompanied the Bichon spoke for the first time. He smiled continuously, with a fixed, artificial grin. Although he looked Chinese, his accent was very confidently American. "Now what Princess Gem means," he said, gesturing to the Bichon, "is that we all need to be very sure of our positions before we continue. It's so we know why we are all here and what we all want from this meeting." He rubbed his hand over his bald head.

"Hmm, *si*," agreed Carlos. "Well, I 'ave kept-a my side of de bargain. I 'ave organised de destruction of vast amounts of chocolate in de UK, wit lots of chocolate shops raided. I 'ave also started de distribution of your-a cheap alternative, so dat people can get hooked on dat instead. De Great Gabâ owes-a me a lot-a money. Ha!"

"Very well," said Princess Gem. "You will get some of your money. The job isn't finished yet. The chocolate shops will soon recover, and we need to know that the chocolate business in the UK is closed down permanently. You must organise more raids and keep on raiding until our own bar, Choccy Yum, is the *only* chocolate bought in the UK."

"That's easy, boss," growled Boris. "We can just keep sending the gangs out on their stolen mobility scooters, an' tell them they are doing the work of the Great Gabâ. They love it!"

"Yes, as long as you keep paying us. But we cannot-a do dis forever," said Carlos. "I tort dat-a de price agreed was for just de one job. Who is dis Great Gabâ, anyway, and why isn't 'ee 'ere? What 'as-a 'ee got against chocolate?"

"Ah, yes," said Princess Gem gently. "Lots of questions, quite understandable. Mr Yan, please explain for our guests."

"Where shall I start?" asked the smartly dressed man, learning forward in his seat. "First, the Great Gabâ. The Great Gabâ will never come to meet you. He is too great; he lives on the island of Bohol in the Philippines and never leaves. He has endless reserves of money and only wants to use it for good. You see," continued the man after taking a sip of his drink and looking around the table, "cacao plants, from which all chocolate is made, have a quite rare position on the globe. They only grow in particular places, in the tropics of the world, where temperature, humidity and rainfall all stay the same throughout the year. The Philippines, where we find the island of Bohol, is quite new to cacao growing, and only started in the 1980s. Now, it is the third leading producer of cocoa beans. It is a growing business! There is more money and more people coming to the Great Gabâ's island." The man stopped for everyone to take in this information.

"And surely dis-a is a good thing? De people of Bohol, dey must love it?" Carlos asked, now interested.

"Yes, the people do," Mr Yan said firmly. "For the Great Gabâ, though, this is a bad thing. He does not want people or their money coming to and taking over his beautiful Chocolate Hills or poaching endangered animals. Global warming and climate change are caused by humans. It is affecting all animals. It cannot be stopped. Bohol is one of the important cocoa growing places that's now becoming very important. The Great Gabâ wants people to stop eating chocolate and start eating his Choccy Yum bars. His great work has started in the UK. It is one of the places in the world where most chocolate is eaten."

"But won't people still want-a de chocolate?" Carlos asked.

"No," Mr Yan replied. "Choccy Yum might not taste as good as chocolate, but it has a special ingredient, making it very addictive."

"And to begin with," Princess Gem continued, pausing to stick out her pink tongue and lick her nose, "it will be very cheap. As soon as you have organised for it to be impossible to buy real chocolate again, we will put the price up and be very rich. Choccy Yum is very cheap for us to make too."

She put out a paw to her big security guard and he reached inside his jacket pocket, producing a Choccy Yum bar. He put it down on the table. I glanced across at the table from behind the pillar to see the bar. It was just like the ones we saw at the airport. Its green and orange striped wrapper with the big black letters across the front saying Choccy Yum now seemed quite scary, having heard more about it.

"Choccy Yum has no nutritional value," said Mr Yan. "It will not fill you up, it doesn't taste particularly great – just a bit chocolatey – but it's very addictive. It's just full of chemicals, special addictive chemicals that, once tasted, people just want more and more of. Would you like to try some? I wouldn't recommend it."

"No fanks!" shouted Boris. "It sounds rubbish."

"Oh, it is!" agreed Princess Gem. "But it will make us rich. As long as you do as we ask. And, of course, all of your gangs keep following the wishes of the Great Gabâ, risking their own health, poor things. All in the hope of a better life. Fools. This Great Gabâ story has worked so far it seems. Hee hee!" she giggled.

"You mean, de Great Gabâ doesn't really exist?" Carlos asked, sounding a little puzzled.

"Well," said Princess Gem, smiling and glancing across at Mr Yan. "This version, of an Indonesian traditional story, does. There perhaps once was a Great Gabâ, but when we heard of it, we used his story. We changed it so that we can control other weak animals. It suits our purposes. Now I insist that you both try a little bit of Choccy Yum. It is important to know what you are selling."

Carlos and Boris looked alarmed and were about to protest, but Princess Gem continued. "Now don't worry about becoming addicted, because here is the antidote!"

She looked over to Mr Yan, who raised his hand in a signal to the barman. The barman quickly brought a tray with a single glass of a dark brown liquid over to the table. He then gave a little bow and went back to the bar again.

"Yuck!" Boris exclaimed. "That looks grim."

Mr Yan said, "Once you have tasted Choccy Yum, you will instantly want more and more. One sip of this, however, and you will be cured. It's just prune juice. Plain and simple prune juice. It's an easy cure but a complete secret. Not many people drink prune juice so they are not going to discover it."

"Hmm," Carlos said doubtfully. "Okay den, break off a bit. Let's try it. Boris, eat it!" he ordered.

Boris opened his mouth and tipped his head back. Mr Yan broke off a little piece and threw it up across the table, and Boris caught it in his mouth. In a second, he had swallowed it. They all waited to see what would happen.

"Blimey!" Boris said. "It's really bad; it's a bit chocolatey, I suppose. Just chemicals, you say? Hmm. Actually, it's not bad at all. In fact, could I just have a bit more? Or maybe not just a bit. Maybe just give me the whole bar. In fact…" Boris demanded, quite forcefully now "…give me the whole bar now. I want it; give it to me!" He stood in his seat and leaned forward aggressively. The security dog stiffened but waited for orders before he attacked. Boris was sounding quite vicious now and was about to jump down from his seat, to take the bar of Choccy Yum.

"Stop!" ordered Carlos. "Stop at once, Boris. Now-a look, Mr Yan is coming round to you, to pour a little of de prune juice down-a your troat, so open wide."

As soon as the prune juice had been administered by Mr Yan, Boris instantly calmed down. He could visibly be seen to relax back into his chair, and he sighed contentedly.

"Well, I'm impressed," Carlos admitted. "*Molto impressionato!* In fact, a great-a demonstration. But 'ere is some-ting important dat 'as me confused. If Choccy Yum is so addictive, why-a did we do all de chocolate raids? Couldn't you 'ave just started selling Choccy Yum? People would-a soon be 'ooked on it."

"That is true," agreed Princess Gem, nodding slowly. "But we needed to have the chocolate raids to start the whole thing off. I know that Choccy Yum is very addictive and very cheap, but it doesn't taste that good. Most people wouldn't even try a chocolate-flavoured candy bar to start with, if they could get hold of affordable real chocolate."

Everyone in the group gently nodded as they all understood this.

"Secondly, your earlier point was right. The chocolate raids will not go on forever and eventually the chocolate production will recover. We have to ensure that people don't just go back to eating normal proper chocolate again. After all, it tastes much better than Choccy Yum!"

All of the criminals smiled around at each other.

"*Concordato!*" said Carlos, in Italian, jumping down from his chair and coming over to lick Mr Yan and Princess Gem on the cheeks. "I agree wid your plan!" Their security man and dog stiffened up again, wondering what he was doing.

"It sound-a like a great plan, so let's shake on it. Now send-a me de money and we are all systems go! I-a will do anything for money, if de price is right. You must send it all now. Ha!"

"We have just sent the *first* instalment," said Princess Gem softly. "We have started selling Choccy Yum as well, in airports. We just needed to make sure of your commitment to our project. However, I really would recommend that you turn around and look at the light show."

Jeff and I turned around too. It was quite dark now. All the tall skyscrapers along the bank of Hong Kong's Victoria Harbour were lit up in an amazing display of lights and laser beams. The buildings flashed and pulsed with moving illuminations, and bright lasers criss-crossed in the velvety dark sky.

As I sat up in my seat and scratched at my fur, I thought about what I had just heard. All done in the name of the Great Gabâ? It was easy to dismiss all this simply as an idea just to make money from selling cheap fake chocolate. But I thought there must be more to it. I said this to Jeff.

"They seemed to say that the Great Gabâ isn't real. I'm not sure, though. All the animals in Britain seem quite convinced that he is real."

"I agree with you, Ned," Jeff said, turning briefly from looking at the lights. "Well, you know what we need to do now then, don't you?"

"What?" I asked, also mesmerised by the flashing brightness across the harbour.

"We need to meet the Great Gabâ and find out what this is all about. Let's try to follow those two new criminals, 'cos I bet they are going back to meet him."

We turned to where the party of criminals had been sitting. Their table was empty. Whilst we had been watching the light show, they had disappeared.

CHAPTER 15
TOO MUCH

The Great Gabâ and his gang had planned perhaps their most audacious robbery yet. They had left their home, near to the Chocolate Hills, and were all holding on tight with their strong fingers. They were on the top of a bus that was travelling to the Integrated Bus Terminal at Island City Mall. Being so small, the tarsiers had no fear of being spotted. It was the last bus of the day, so the light was fading fast. At nighttime, tarsiers really wake up.

"Hey, Dink… I mean, Great Gabâ," called one of the tarsier gang, shouting across the roof of the rumbling bus. "What is it we are all going to Tagbilaran for? I know you told us we must all do as we are told, but it does seem a very long way."

"You'd better all listen carefully, gang," answered Dinky. "We are going to our capital city because that's the place *where it's at!*" He said this last bit in a New York sort of accent because he was trying to sound all gangster and 'street'.

Dinky looked around at his five other gang members. They were all clinging to the roof bars. He could see all their large eyes looking at him in the fading light. "We all need mobile phones, right?"

The gang all answered in one voice, "Right!"

"And Tagbilaran is a busy place with lots of people, right?"

"Right!" the gang answered.

"And tarsiers, with our super strong fingers, small bodies, and our superb ability to see in the dark make excellent pickpockets, perfect for stealing phones, right?"

"Right!" they all answered.

"Yeah, but why are we all going to Tagbilaran?" asked one of the tarsiers, nearly overbalancing as the bus went over a bump in the road.

"Surely, you're not serious," Dinky groaned. "I give up! I thought I'd just explained that. Look, just follow orders, okay? We're here now, so as soon as the bus stops, we're going to jump off and hide until all the people have gone. Okay, get ready… and go!"

The bus came to a standstill, but before the doors opened, the tarsiers climbed down the side until it was safe to jump. Dinky indicated that they should all follow him and took them behind a nearby crate.

"Now what, boss?" a tarsier asked, who was hidden in the shadows.

"When no one is watching, we are going to sneak

into the Island City shopping mall, which is just next door. We shall commit what shall become known as the 'Great Phone Robbery!' People will be talking about this momentous time for years to come!"

"But, Great Gabâ," said another more sensible gang member, "there are only six of us, right? And we can't possibly steal more than one phone each. Mobile phones are as big as we are, if not bigger."

"And your point is…?" said Dinky, angrily. Until now, he had been rather proud of his plan.

"Well, it won't ever really be known as the Great Phone Robbery, will it? I mean, six phones is not really a *great* number. There could be hundreds of people in the mall right now and six phones going missing, I mean to say—"

"Right! Enough!" interrupted Dinky. "Enough talking, let's get to work, guys, and do our *thang!*"

"Our what, Gaba?"

"Oh, let's just go," Dinky said wearily, leading the way to the shopping mall.

Five minutes later, the gang had all come out again. They did indeed have a phone, but they didn't really steal it. They had found it on the pavement outside the bus station, where someone had dropped it.

The gang had all managed to enter the mall. It was getting dark outside and was all relatively quiet, but Dinky hadn't banked on the different conditions inside the mall. They had all sneaked through together as someone held a door open for their child. As soon as the group entered, they all wished that they hadn't. The lights! They were so bright! When you have eyes as large as a tarsier's, bright lights in a shopping mall can be almost blinding.

Next, there was the noise.

Tarsiers have very sensitive hearing. The high volume of the music that was played into the mall, together with the noise of everyone talking and shouting, was too much for even Dinky to bear.

Keeping their heads down and waiting for the next opportunity to occur, they crouched down in the shadows next to the door. Dinky didn't even shout, "Go!" when the door was held open again; they just all ran as fast as they could out into the darkness and quiet of the night.

"When's the next bus home, boss?" asked one of the gang, all excitement gone from his voice now. Dinky knew they would have to wait now until tomorrow night. Unless…

Dinky leant against the one phone that they had managed to 'steal', that now stood propped against the wall. At least it was a smartphone. It wasn't locked and had lots of credit. It was in one of those cases that had a flap that folded over the screen at the front. The person who had owned the phone had also kept their money tucked into the little pocket in the front flap.

"Let's go home now," Dinky said, to the surprise of his gang. "We'll take a taxi."

CHAPTER 16
BLOW OUT

I stepped into the waiting lift and turned around to see my reflection in the mirrors, which were on the back of the closing doors. We had just left the highest bar in the world and were now making our way out of the building.

"Which button do you think I press?" asked my person.

"The one with the lowest number on it. We are leaving the top floor and trying to get down to the ground again."

"Okay, there we go. We're on our way down from Ozone to the ground, well, at least to the middle lobby first. Hold on to your tummy!" exclaimed Jeff.

"What do you think about what we just heard up there?" I asked. "This Great Gabâ, do you think he is real? I got the feeling that they might just be making him up, as a way to trick the stray dogs into doing their dirty work for them."

My tummy did feel a bit funny as we descended from the one hundred and eighteenth floor, but we were soon down to the halfway point and the door opened again, so that we could walk out into the white and shiny lobby. We silently walked over to the other lift that would take us down to the ground. The building was so tall that the lift needed to be in two stages.

When the lift doors closed behind us, we continued our conversation.

"Yes, I kind of agree," said Jeff. "But what if he *is* real? We have been asked to find out, and there is only one way to do that. We need to go to Bohol, wherever that may be! We'll need to get Gizzmo to check on Poodle Maps."

We eventually reached the ground and the lift doors opened onto the main foyer. Across the busy crowds of humans, dogs and cats, I thought I caught a glimpse of a small and thin Italian Greyhound accompanied by a large hairy-looking Boris. My heart gave a lurch of fear as I was sure that he turned briefly to look at us, over his shoulder. He might recognise us from London. I hoped our disguises would work.

"Quick, there they are!" I exclaimed. "We need to get after them."

I started forward, but someone said, "Stop, chaps!"

The words came from Jeff, but it wasn't him. I turned to look. The voice continued talking and I realised that it was coming from Jeff's pocket.

"You have left *MI5 Can Hear You* switched on, and I can hear every word!" I then recognised the voice as that of the man behind the newspaper. Jeff and I quickly darted to the edge of the reception area and stood behind another large tree in a pot.

"I can hear every word, chaps," said the man behind the newspaper. "And there will be no need to follow the blighters any more for now; we certainly have enough evidence to arrest them all, thanks to your recording. We are going to pass this information on to Interpol, the International Police. The people at the meeting are all known cheats, who are wanted in lots of countries. Interpol will do the arresting."

"What about us then?" Jeff asked, hoping that this great adventure was not over yet.

"Oh, you chaps haven't finished by a long shot!"

Jeff and I looked at each other and smiled, feeling excited again.

"Off to Bohol you go, and find out about this Gabâ character. He is still a 'person of interest', as we say. If he does really exist, then he jolly well needs to be stopped! Now get back to your hotel, get your things, and have a word with Gizzmo on the way. Get her to book you a flight to Bohol. We can't hang about chatting, you know!" he ordered.

Coming out from behind the large tree in a pot, we went out through the front doors. We climbed into one of the many waiting taxis and showed the driver the address of the hotel on Jeff's phone. The driver sped through the busy roads of Kowloon, across one of the bridges, to the even busier streets of Hong Kong Island. Here we became stuck in congested traffic.

Jeff used his phone to video call Gizzmo. This time she was back in her usual place in The Sticky Bun café, her wide cup of Flat Bright next to her.

"Dudes!" she exclaimed delightedly, obviously pleased to see us. "You're alive! Hey, my spy-type pals! How did it all go? Have you guys solved the chocolate mystery yet? Who did it?"

"That's loads of questions, Gizzmo!" I said as I put my front paws up on my person to get a better view of the smartphone. "And we will answer them all eventually. First, though, you need to help us again."

"Of course, dude! Consider it already done! Er… what is it that you want done?"

"Well," said Jeff, brushing some of my hairs from his trousers onto the floor of the taxi. "Firstly, can you find out where Bohol is?"

He slowly peeled off his false moustache now as we spoke, wincing a bit as he pulled against the very sticky glue that had held the disguise firmly to his face. The taxi driver looked back at us in his rear-view mirror and I could see his forehead furrow and his eyes widen in surprise.

"I don't need to check for you, dude!" interrupted Gizzmo. "I already know. It's in the Philippines. It's one of the many islands, and it's popular with tourist-type dudes. Hey, you guys should leave that most excellent face furniture on," she protested as I too pulled at my fake moustache. "I really think that you two dudes have found your new essential look."

"But it's really itchy, Gizzmo," I answered. "I'll take it off carefully and use it again another time."

"Okay, good," Jeff said. "You know where the place is, so we can find out more later on. The second thing is, we need to go there. Can you book us some transport please, using the MI5 credit card again? You have all the details, don't you? Apparently, it needs to be as soon as possible."

"No worries, dudes," said Gizzmo. "As you can see, I'm already searching on my laptop. I'll text you the details of the bookings and where you need to go."

We heard the tap of the computer keys as Gizzmo closed the video call connection. I tried to relax for a few minutes, listening to the sound of the driver chatting to someone non-stop on his phone, in Chinese. There were no animal seatbelts in these Hong Kong taxis, so Jeff held me tightly as we swayed around corners.

I glanced out of my window and saw that in the lane beside us was a man peddling very quickly, on a bicycle. It was an old-fashioned bicycle and the man was dressed in a traditional Chinese working man's loose brown smock and three-quarter length trousers. He also wore a pair of white Converse trainers. He sometimes had to pedal quite fast to keep up with the traffic, although he often put one foot down to stop as the congested traffic ground to a halt again. What was most extraordinary was that sitting upright in a basket on the handlebars of the bicycle was a small white and fluffy cat. The cat was pure white and looked similar to the 'Hello Kitty' children's toy. The cat seemed very relaxed about all the frantically busy, beeping traffic that surrounded him. He even appeared to have his eyes closed and was permanently grinning. I poked Jeff with my nose and told him to turn and look too.

"What has that cat got in his mouth, gripped between his teeth?" he asked, leaning over me to get a better look.

"It's a matchstick!" I exclaimed. "One of those with a red match head that you can strike on any surface."

"The man riding the bike doesn't seem to be in the least bit puffed out, even though he needs to peddle quite fast," Jeff observed. "What are those two big gas cylinders in that rack on the front of the bike? What a strange way to transport gas. Whoa!" he suddenly said in alarm. "I can see now that it says 'acetylene gas' on the side of them, it's got one of those 'explosive' warning signs too. That's the gas they use for welding metal. That doesn't seem very safe. I wouldn't like to be that cat!"

"No way," I said, fidgeting uncomfortably in my person's arms as the taxi moved on. "They don't seem to have the same health and safety laws that we do at home. I wish that we could move on and be a bit further away from them. They keep coming close to us and it doesn't feel very safe!"

The traffic stopped again and we paused beside one of the incredible basket works of bamboo-scaffolding that covered the front of a building that was being repaired. The bamboo poles were only tied together with rope, but they were amazingly high. They looked rickety to me, but there were men working from them without harnesses. They were climbing around and confidently swinging on the poles to get to the high parts of the building.

I was about to comment on the daredevil scaffolders, when the cat on the bicycle pulled up beside us again as we stopped. Jeff tutted as he noticed too.

At that moment, the chatter of the taxi driver that had been non-stop since we had left the Ritz-Carlton, went quiet. I looked up and saw with alarm that the driver was opening his door and throwing himself out onto the road. Who had he been on the phone to?

What took place next must have only taken a few seconds, but to me it all seemed like slow motion. I heard a hiss of gas beside me and smelt a strange garlicky smell. I turned around to see that the man on the bicycle had shoved a pipe through the open window. He was using it to deliver gas from his cylinders into our taxi, filling the inside of the car. The cat was now facing us and still happily grinning. Jeff looked too; he suddenly realised what must be happening. He fumbled for the handle of his door, desperately trying to open it. I carried on watching with horror as the man on the bicycle leaned forward and took the match from the grinning cat's mouth. The cat ducked a little as the match was struck on his head. The wooden stick was held still for a second, to allow the flame to catch alight properly.

"Come on, get out!" I shouted. "The cat is trying to blow us up!"

At that moment, Jeff had the door open and grabbed me tightly. He pulled me across and flung me out of the stationary vehicle, tumbling out behind. We looked back as we heard what sounded like a Chinese swear word from the bicycle-riding man.

"His match must have gone out," gasped Jeff. "We need to get out of here quick!"

The would-be bombers must have changed their minds on realising we weren't in the taxi anymore; they cycled off through the traffic. Cars behind us beeped loudly, as our taxi now stayed still whilst all the other lanes of traffic moved on.

"Let's not hang about," remarked Jeff, scrabbling up to his feet. "Up here, look, away from the road, I'll help you."

He gestured towards one of the wooden ladders that went up to the scaffolding and, lifting me up under one arm, he climbed the short ladder up to the first level that we could walk on. As soon as my paws touched the wooden walkway, we both ran along the bouncing and unsteady planks, towards the other end of the building. The workmen were shouting and waving for us to get off, but we frantically ran on.

This was not a good idea. The white cat, followed by the cycling man, had also climbed the scaffolding from the other end. They had seen what we were doing from the road and were now coming towards us.

"Aargh!" I let out a cry of alarm. "We need to go up again. Quickly, pick me up like you did before."

Jeff picked me up under his arm and started climbing. This ladder stuck out at many points and was tied on frayed bits of rope.

"Keep climbing," I gasped. Jeff's grip was tight, as he needed to keep me safe, but it made it hard to breathe. "They are following us up!"

The bicycle-riding man had the grinning white cat sitting calmly on his shoulder whilst he climbed the ladders. He was a lot quicker than Jeff, having both his hands free.

"I'm going to have to put you down," Jeff croaked, as he breathlessly dropped me onto another one of the creaky scaffolding boards.

We seemed really high up now. We were six floors above the road but it felt much higher as the scaffolding was swaying. It creaked and groaned worryingly.

"Over at the end," I puffed as we made our way carefully along the thin plank, "I see one of those yellow plastic chutes that the workmen throw the building rubbish into. It takes the rubble safely down to a skip on the ground."

"Oh no," said Jeff. "You are not seriously suggesting that we throw ourselves down there?"

"That's exactly what I am suggesting," I answered, now getting close to the chute's round opening. "Have you got another plan?"

Jeff looked behind him at our pursuers, who were now also on our scaffolding level. They were quickly making their way towards us. Jeff's answer was to take one look at the chute's entrance and throw himself head first into the yellow tunnel. I waited a second for Jeff to start his descent and headed after him.

The chute was quite light inside, but it moved and rattled as our weight pushed it out of shape. We dropped quickly. The chute curved upwards very slightly as it approached the skip, and this was just enough to slow our fall. Even so, we were both dumped heavily into the skip, amongst all the dust, rubbish and building materials. It took a few moments for me to recover.

"Now what?" I coughed. "The cat will be down here in a minute."

"I dunno," responded Jeff sullenly, climbing out of the skip. "The chute was your 'brilliant' plan."

"We need to get lost among the crowds," I said, jumping down onto the roadside. "This place looks extremely busy; it's a shopping mall." I pointed my nose at an automatic door that was opening and closing as different animals and people went into the mall next to us. Jeff looked puzzled for a moment but must have understood my plan as he didn't argue and just went on through the entrance. He led me into all the crowds and queues. We went in as far as we could, ignoring the annoyed looks and protests of the shoppers as we barged past them. Only then did we look back through the glass doors.

We saw the cycling man and then the cat, still grinning, pop out of the chute as we had done. They stood up on the rubbish, to see where we had gone. We couldn't be seen from the skip, and there was no clue that we had hidden behind the crowds in the mall. The pair carried on searching for a few more minutes. The man shook his head at the grinning cat and the two of them hopped out of the skip. The cat quickly glanced into the mall entrance, but they made their way off in the other direction. They were clearly baffled by our sudden disappearance.

The cool air conditioning calmed me down, and I felt able to think straight again.

"We can walk back to our hotel from here," said Jeff. "I recognise this from when we walked down to the ferry, but I think we should wait here for a bit."

"Well, it's time for a Flat Bright," I suggested, and I sat down at an empty table next to a little Chihuahua and her tiny pup. "I think we both need to calm down a little first."

"I'm still shaking as I think about what nearly happened there," said Jeff, sitting beside me. "If that gas from those cylinders had caught alight, the grinning cat and half of the building next to us would have been blown up too!"

"That grinning cat was clearly crazy," I commented. "Perhaps the Great Gabâ had told them to do it.

Someone out there doesn't want us to share what we know about them. This must be a cheating operation that's worth big money." I paused and shuffled back in my seat, trying to catch the busy Poodle dog waitress' attention. I caught sight of a very big lucky golden cat statue, which was waving with one paw and dominating the space in the mall. It made me think about how lucky we had been that the match did not light. I gulped and was eager to change the unhappy mood that we were both in. "I know something that will cheer you up," I said, grinning. "It's another one of my cat jokes. If that crazy cat had succeeded in its evil plan, do you know what it would have been? It would have been a 'cat-astrophe'!"

CHAPTER 17
THRILLER IN MANILA

By the time we had got our things together at the hotel and checked out of our room, Gizzmo had sent us the details. The flight left in about three hours so we needed to jump straight into another taxi. I had a quick toilet-stop first. We went back to the metro railway station and then to the airport.

"This jet-set lifestyle is going to be the death of me!" declared Jeff as we stood in yet another airport queue. "I just can't cope with this fast pace. I'm still shaking from earlier on. It's nighttime, remember, and I don't think we are going to get much sleep."

"Hmm," I replied, deep in thought. "We'll have to try and grab a few minutes' sleep on the plane. The criminal gang knows that we are here. They must have seen us as we left the Ritz-Carlton building."

"True," agreed Jeff as we took another couple of shuffling steps forward in the airport queue. "But so what? We are going to another country now. The man behind the newspaper said Interpol would arrest them."

"But they haven't been arrested yet," I replied, shuffling forward again. "What if they are still looking for us? What if they try to kidnap us again? Or worse!"

"Worse than being buried under a few tons of concrete in a cellar in London? Or worse than being blown up in a Hong Kong taxi?" Jeff exclaimed. "How much worse can it get?"

I gave him a hard stare. "My point is, that it is a good idea, before we get through the check-in desk, security and show our passports, to be in disguise again. I'm thinking that now might be the right time to use our *other* passports. To become 'John' and 'Nedmondo'. Just as a precaution."

Our friends must have had the same thoughts, because Jeff's phone beeped, showing us he had a text message. It was from Gizzmo. It said: *Hey, dudes! Big soz, 'cos I forgot to tell you that your tickets are booked in your undercover disguise names of Nedmondo and John. You'll need to change to look like your passport photos. The dude behind the newspaper told me to do this. He was worried you might be being looked for. Have fun, dudes!*

"I think that you rather fancy the idea of becoming 'Nedmondo,'" said Jeff. "I think a moustache suits you. You'll have to reapply the hair dye on your fur, though. Nedmondo is a different colour from you, remember."

"I know," I replied. "This queue is moving really slowly, so I'll have plenty of time to nip off to the toilets over there and rub myself all over with hair dye. I'll hold the bottle in my mouth, pour some out over the tiled floor, then roll around in it like I do when we are out for a walk sometimes, getting a smell on me."

"Oh, you dirty dog!" laughed Jeff. "Yes, you do like to roll round in filthy things on our walks and you do manage to get yourself completely covered. Look, here's the bottle then. I'll stick the moustache on you when you get back. I'll keep our place in the queue. You'll have to look out for me, though, because I'm not going to be able to recognise you if you are a different colour!"

"As soon as I get back, you go off to the toilet too. You need to stick your moustache on and it'll be easier if you look in the mirror."

With that, I took the bottle of hair dye that Jeff handed to me in my mouth and went off to change the colour of my fur, from white with tan patches, to a yellowy Golden Retriever colour.

When I came back to the queue, Jeff had moved a lot further up. He stuck my moustache onto me.

"Your turn now," I said. "Wait a minute, though, I've just remembered. You are supposed to be clean-shaven, and you are not wearing glasses on your passport photo."

"Oh no!" Jeff exclaimed. "You're right, I totally forgot. I haven't got time to put some contact lenses in now. I'm sure other people who have glasses aren't wearing them on their passport photos. In fact, I'm sure that you are supposed to take them off when you have your photo taken. It'll be okay. Let's just be confident. You look great, though," he said, looking down at my newly dyed fur. "I think you should stay like that. You've done a good job this time."

"Aw, thanks!" I replied sarcastically as he jogged to the toilets.

He was back soon, and it was our turn at the desk next. I felt worried, and I could see Jeff was too. We would be in serious trouble if we were found out. What we were doing was illegal. I looked over at Jeff in his fake moustache. He had the same style of 'face furniture' as I did. The moustaches were of the wide variety and stuck out from the side of our faces. We looked a bit like World War One fighter pilots. We looked ridiculous. It was all I could do to not run away. I thought, *What a stupid idea, whoever thought that this would—?*

"Excuse me!" the shiny black cat said on the check-in desk. She was assisted by a small, spiky-haired man, who looked very serious. "Excuse me!" she said again, interrupting my train of thought. "Your passports are all in order. May I ask, did you pack your bags yourself? Yes? You can proceed to the departure lounge and watch the gate numbers; your flight departs in two hours. Have a great day! Next, please…"

"Wow, we did it!" I exclaimed in delight and relief. "Our disguises worked!"

Jeff was equally pleased, and equally surprised.

"I don't mind admitting that I felt a bit worried there, especially looking over at you and thinking how silly you looked!" he grinned.

When the gate noticeboard showed our gate number, we made our way on board the aeroplane. This aircraft was not as big as the one we were on last time and was arranged differently inside, with only one central aisle down the middle of the plane.

We were sitting comfortably, with extra legroom for Jeff, extra 'curl-up' room for me and a drink each. I asked my person a question that had been worrying me these last few hours.

"When we get to Bohol—"

"Yeah, we have to fly to Manila first, and then catch another flight to the island of Bohol," he interrupted.

"Yes, but when we get there," I continued, "and we have to find the Great Gabâ, how are we going to know where to search and how will we know what he, or she, looks like when we find them?"

There was silence for a few minutes whilst he thought about this, twiddling his new moustache. The flight attendant brought us some more drinks, and of course some food, and then he answered.

"I've been thinking about all that we know about the Great Gabâ. Everyone who has spoken about him has referred to him as a 'he', so we know that much. He is really famous too – even people and animals as far away as England have heard about him, so I'm sure that anyone we ask will be able to direct us to him. And finally, he sounds like a big and powerful figure. You never know, he might find us first! He sounds quite frightening, actually."

"He does," I agreed. "I guess we'll just have to wait and see, and be brave."

Manila Airport was a complete contrast to the calm and organised Hong Kong Airport. There were queues of animals and people everywhere and it was hard to find how we were supposed to get to our connecting flight to Bohol. We had just about given up when Jeff spun around quickly with a little gasp. I looked up to see a large brown and white Beagle whack him on the back of the legs for a second time.

"Hey! Mister!" he called. "I've had to check for travellers from Hong Kong against two sets of photographs, with and without your disguises. They suit you! I've been looking for you for the last hour or so. The man in MI5 thought you might need a little help here. It's a bit busy! Follow me." The Beagle was a jolly friendly local. Even so, we had to take care.

"How do we know he's on our side?" I whispered to my person as we dutifully followed along through the crowds.

"We don't!" he said. "But at the moment we don't have much choice. We are lost anyway; let's see what happens, but stay alert for any funny business."

We kept on going, pushing through different groups who were queuing in big snaking lines as we crossed the sprawling airport.

"This is where you guys want to be," announced our guide, sitting up on his hind legs and spreading his front legs out in welcome. "You are going to find the Great Gabâ in Bohol, right?" he asked as we looked at him blankly with our large moustached faces.

"Oh yes, of course," I replied. "But to tell you the truth, we are just following you and we don't really know who you are. Sorry, I hope I'm not offending you."

The Beagle sat down on the shiny airport floor and laughed.

"Of course I take no offense!" he laughed again. "In fact, it is I who should apologise for not introducing myself properly; it's just that it was so busy over there. I am Armando and I work for the British Government here in Manila. If it helps you trust me more, I know that you're trying to solve the great chocolate mystery and you successfully escaped a dangerous gang of criminals in London, who were trying to bury you under tons of concrete. Well done, by the way."

"Thanks!" I said. "We've had a bit of a 'close shave' in Hong Kong too. Okay, well, when we get to Bohol, can you tell us how we might find this Great Gabâ? If he really exists, that is."

"Oh, he really exists," said Armando. "At least, his reputation really exists. There are a lot of animals worldwide who worship him. He has promised to lead them all to a better life. And to punish the bad humans who have mistreated animals. Gabâ means 'divine retribution' in the original language of the Philippines, before the Spanish took over in the 1520s. In a traditional proverb of the islands, Gabâ is to do with 'bad karma'. If someone does something bad, then something bad will happen to them. I guess you could say that it's a kind of superstition or magic."

"Magic!" I exclaimed, my ears pricking up. "The Great Gabâ exists and he is magic! Well, now I *am* really worried, but very curious too."

"*Huwag Kang mag-alala!*" said our guide. "That means don't worry in Filipino! Gabâ only takes retribution on creatures that have done bad things. You'll be fine!" he laughed again. "Now you'd better get moving or you will miss your plane. Next stop is Tagbilaran, the capital of Bohol. Good luck!" Armando stood up and walked off in the direction of the crowds again, leaving us to walk off in the other direction, towards our next flight.

The aeroplane to Bohol was even smaller than the one that had taken us to Manila, and there was not really any difference between our seats and anyone else's. The flight time was only an hour, and our fellow passengers were mainly tourists, by the look of them. There were dogs and cats of different sizes, and their people were mostly dressed in the colourful Hawaiian-style shirts, which are favoured by people going on holiday to hot countries.

As the aeroplane banked around before landing at Tagbilaran Airport, I got a great view of the beautiful island. It was lush and green, like a jewel set into the turquoise blue of the tropical ocean. I became more excited about our visit, and hoped the dangers were left behind.

CHAPTER 18
CHOCOLATE HILLS

"Dinky! Dinky! Where *have* you been?" shouted Dinky's mum, when she found him at last. "I've been worried sick! I heard some silly story about you being seen clinging onto the roof of a bus with your gang last night. I thought, my Dinky wouldn't be doing a silly thing like that. He's not that silly, is he?"

"No, Mum," replied Dinky. "That would be a very silly thing. No, I was just mucking about at the entrance to one of the caves in the Chocolate Hills, and we just decided to sleep out there today instead of coming all the way back. That's okay, isn't it? I mean, I'm a big tarsier now and I should be taking care of myself, shouldn't I, Mum?" Dinky looked at his mum pleadingly with his huge eyes, his long fingers clasped together in front of him. This always melted his mother's heart.

"Oh, Dinky, how can I be angry with you when you look at me like that? I was just worried, that's all."

"I'm sorry, Mum," Dinky said. "I promise I will tell you where I am going next time."

"You must be careful in those caves in the Chocolate Hills too!" she warned, biting the head off a passing butterfly. "Your father used to spend too much time up there, and look what happened to him. He was seen and taken by those tourists, and that was the last we saw of him." She turned her back and climbed off in search of more insects to eat.

Dinky's gang had only managed to return with one phone that someone had dropped on the pavement. *Never mind*, thought Dinky, it was one more phone that the gang could use to track the movements of tourists.

Dinky believed the tourists deserved lots of bad things to happen to them, after what had been done to his father. It was also one more phone that could be used by the gang to keep the secret safe. Dinky's father's secret, that he had passed on to Dinky for safekeeping.

Dinky swore he would give out retribution for what had happened. That's why he called himself the Great Gabâ. People should be scared. Gabâ was an old word and Dinky felt he was part of that old tradition of the island.

Beneath the Chocolate Hills were many caves. Deep in a particular cave was an amazing secret.

Dinky and his gang were working hard to keep that secret safe, especially as there were more and more tourists coming to Bohol nowadays. He would need to be very vigilant.

CHAPTER 19
TAXI TALK

"This island is just beautiful!" I declared as we got off the aeroplane. The tarmac of the runway, at the bottom of the aeroplane steps, felt very warm under my feet. The tropical air was sticky, so the wind was lovely as it wafted around us in a light breeze.

"Well, as we don't need to go through customs again and show our passports, I might just take off my fake moustache now. It feels uncomfortable again," complained my person, scratching at his stuck-on moustache.

"Of course," I said. "Bohol is an island in the Philippines; we are in the same country as Manila. Keep your moustache on, though. We don't know that it's safe yet, and it's better if your face matches the photo in the passport you are using. Look, let's go through the airport terminal and use the MI5 credit card to get some money out. Then we can buy something to eat. I'm starving! And keep your moustache on," I advised. "It makes you look very wise; you could do with that," I added, smiling, as I teased him.

"Of course I am wise, so follow me!" agreed Jeff, striding out towards the airport terminal with me loafing along behind. "We can also find out how to get to the hotel that Gizzmo has booked for us to stay in. We can ask if they have heard of the Great Gabâ."

I stopped to wee against the wall before we went into the terminal. The toilet facilities for animals on board the flight had been a bit basic, so I had waited until we landed.

The refreshing cool air of the air conditioning system greeted us as we entered the terminal building. It was a pleasant contrast to the tropical heat of outside.

"The quickest way to get to your hotel is to go by taxi," said the pleasant and smiley Dalmatian on the information desk. She pawed a few of the large buttons on her computer keypad and announced that a taxi would be ready for us outside the front of the airport in about twenty minutes.

She looked up at us again and asked, "Is there anything else I can do for you gentlemen today?"

"No, thank you," Jeff said. "Oh, wait a minute, there is just one thing. We are trying to meet up with a friend of ours called Gabâ. Have you heard of him?"

The Dalmatian froze. Her smile dropped. There was an uncomfortable silence that lasted a few seconds.

"You… are friends… with the Great Gabâ?" she said in a slow, shocked voice. "Oh…"

She quickly turned and jumped down from the desk. We heard her claws clattering on the floor as she disappeared around the corner of the terminal hall.

"That went well then!" I commented sarcastically, whilst I scratched at my collar. "It must be your wisdom and charm."

"As well as can be expected, by the looks of it," he answered. "Come on, let's go out the front of the building and wait for the taxi."

After about half an hour, the battered old yellow taxi turned up and clattered to a halt in front of us.

"Sorry I'm a little late!" apologised the driver, but without much conviction. He did have a big smile, though. "I've just been across at the shopping mall over there." He gestured to a large white and grey building. It was across the road from the airport.

The driver was a large middle-aged man. He was dressed very casually in a loose yellow t-shirt, jeans and flip flops. He smelt of burgers, chips and other fast foods that taxi drivers have to eat when they are on the go all the time.

"That's okay," I said, as we climbed into the baking temperature of the taxi. "We need you to take us to this address, please." Jeff showed the driver the address that he had just been getting up on his phone.

"No problem, sirs!" the driver said cheerfully. "It will take about twenty minutes."

Even with the windows down, the temperature stayed the same in the taxi. The air was just blowing round more freely.

"Do you find that you have lots of people from many places in your taxi?" Jeff asked conversationally. "I know lots of tourists visit your beautiful island."

The driver was whistling a tuneless tune to himself as he drove.

"Oh yes, sirs," the driver answered, unnervingly turning his head to speak to us in the back seat, taking his eyes off the road. "Lots of people from many, many places. Lots of dogs, cats, all sorts. Hee hee!" he chuckled, eventually turning his head, so that his eyes were back on the road.

"I am laughing to myself as I am thinking of a fare that I had in my taxi last night."

"Oh yes?" I said. "Why, were they funny?"

The driver turned around again to talk to us, seemingly unconcerned about any oncoming vehicles.

"Oh yes, sirs, very, very funny. It was a group of tarsiers from the Chocolate Hills area of the island."

"Please excuse my ignorance, but I'm not sure what tarsiers are," I said.

"Tarsiers," the driver explained, turning back to the road once more, just in time, as a large lorry was coming towards us, "tarsiers are Bohol monkeys. They are tiny, tiny creatures. They would fit in the palm of my hand!" He demonstrated the size by showing us his palm, letting go of the steering wheel at the same time. "Well, I should *no*t say they are monkeys. They are relatives of monkeys, I suppose. They are of the primate family? Yes? You know primates?"

"Yes," I confirmed. "Primates."

"They have very, very big eyes, very cute. Their eyes are bigger than their brains. They cannot turn their eyes; instead, they must turn their head! Long, strong fingers, though. Like I said, very, very cute."

"I bet the tourists love them," I said.

"Oh yes," he answered. "Many tourists come just for the tarsier, and to see the Chocolate Hills, of course."

"Aww," Jeff said. "I bet people just want to take the tarsiers home with them, if they are that cute," he joked.

"Well, that is the problem!" shouted out the driver, now becoming very animated and taking both hands off the wheel. "That is why the tarsiers are now a protected species and have their own tarsier sanctuary. There are not the same animal rights and laws as you have in Britain. Do you know what happens to a tarsier if he is taken away from his beloved Bohol?" he asked, now not paying any attention to driving at all, turning around to face us and kneeling up in his seat.

"Ah, no!" I said, feeling a little unsafe.

"Well, it is a terrible thing. He ends his own life. It is just too distressing for him; he cannot cope. He bangs his little head against something hard."

Leaving us with that terrible thought, he turned back around in his seat and took control of the car once more. There was then a few minutes of silence in the car, which the driver filled by humming tunelessly to himself.

"Well, what happened to the tarsiers in your taxi?" Jeff asked, eager to change the mood.

"Oh yes! Ha! They were funny little fellows. Yes, very, very funny. There was a little group of them, five or six. They told me that they had got the bus down to the mall from the Chocolate Hills earlier that evening, but they did not like the bright lights and loud music and now wanted to go home again! See, a tarsier does not like being away from his home. Hee!"

"Oh, I can't wait to meet one," I said. "And the Chocolate Hills, why are they called that?"

The driver finished cleaning out his ear with his little finger and turned his head around once more.

"At this time of year, when it is nice and warm," he said, "the grass that grows there is dry and turns brown, the colour of chocolate. The hills are this shape." He faced the front but used both hands to demonstrate the little mound shapes of each hill. "And they all cluster together like this." Now he bumped his hands up and down repeatedly. "They are said to look like the American chocolate, Hershey, you know? The one called 'Kisses', yes?" He smiled at us again and turned back towards the road.

I said I got the idea and thanked him for the information. He said that we were approaching the end of our journey, and indeed up ahead, clustering in amongst the tropical forest trees, was a group of white and wood-coloured buildings. The driver turned off the road towards them and in less than a minute we were there.

"Now, you fellows," the jolly driver said, sticking his arm out of the window and brushing off his dusty old taxi, "you are not here looking for the lost Japanese gold, are you?"

"No!" I replied, puzzled by his question. "Why do you ask that?"

"Oh, it is nothing," he laughed. "I ask all the visitors that. There are lots of tales about people though history, including the Japanese soldiers in World War Two, hiding gold in the caves under the Chocolate Hills." The driver opened his taxi door with a loud creak and stuck a leg into the sunshine.

"And has any ever been found?" Jeff asked. He opened the old doors and we climbed out onto the dusty road.

"No, no, no!" the driver laughed again. He took the money that Jeff offered to him and stuffed it into his trouser pocket. "But that hasn't stopped many people trying; cave explorers and some such. It is just a good story. Some of the caves are sacred, special places to the local people. Special permission is needed to go there. Anyway, enjoy Bohol!" he called as he jumped in properly and drove away in a cloud of dust.

Once we had checked in at the reception desk (remembering to use our 'moustache' passports to help avoid detection) and gone up to the hotel room, we both laid down on the large bed and let out a happy sigh. The fan on the ceiling above us swept around, pushing cool air down towards our recumbent, sweaty bodies. Well, Jeff was sweaty. Dogs don't sweat. I just stuck out my tongue and panted. The shutters opened onto a large balcony, and the intense green view of the tropical rainforest was perfectly framed by the clean white surround of the wooden slatted walls.

Our rest was, of course, short-lived.

"What ho, chaps!" said the man behind the newspaper on the video call that spoilt our rest.

We both sat on the edge of the bed to talk to him. Although we could still only see his gloved hands holding the newspaper, and the top of his hat, we could also read the front page headline of the newspaper. He changed the newspaper regularly, to complete his disguise. It said, *Chocolate Robberies Still a Mystery.* The subheading said, *Cheap Choccy Yum Becomes the Snack of Choice.*

"I see that you two are reading the headlines in the paper," he said.

We looked at each other and mouthed silently, "How does he know that?"

"Hmm, well, what do you think of that, eh? Nasty business for you in Hong Kong. That cat was a trained assassin, a Ninja. You chaps were lucky to escape, but I knew you were up to the job. Now, the faster you find Gabâ and put a stop to this nonsense, then the sooner everything can get back to normal. So, what are you doing about it?"

We told him everything that we had discovered, from the Beagle at Manila Airport and the reaction of the Dalmatian when we landed in Bohol to the information from the taxi driver.

"You're no closer to Gabâ, though, are you? So, enough lying around on your bed! Get out and find him, before the entire population of Britain has forgotten what real chocolate tastes like. They will all be addicted to Choccy Yum soon."

We both stood up as he broke the connection, and Jeff bent down to brush all the hairs that I had left on the bed off onto the floor.

"I really don't know where to start, now that we are here," admitted Jeff, sounding puzzled. "Lots of people know about Gabâ, it seems, but they don't know where we can find him."

"I know what will cheer us up, and perhaps give us a bit of thinking time," I suggested. "Let's go up to the Chocolate Hills and maybe stop off on the way to see some little tarsier monkeys. I'd love to see one while we are here."

"Good idea, Ned. I'll ask at the hotel reception about how we do that. By the way, did you notice that we are both still wearing our false moustaches? I'm getting quite used to mine now!"

I turned to look at myself in the mirror on the wall. I did look quite dashing, if I say so myself.

CHAPTER 20
MAGIC SECRETS

Dinky stood beside the cave entrance and waited patiently for the rest of his gang to arrive. They had all arranged to meet here, but Dinky had come a little early as he wanted time to be alone for a while.

There were many caves under the Chocolate Hills, and some were being explored by tourists and cave explorers. The caves varied in size, from quite small to large and impressive. They were formed when the water that passes through the limestone of the hills cuts out caverns and tunnels of different sizes, leaving little springs and rivers.

But this cave was different. It was certainly not the grandest, but it contained something very special. This was the whole reason that Dinky thought he should be called the Great Gabâ.

Dinky had inherited this title from his father really, but the reason was that he was the guardian of magic.

"Hey, Dinks… I mean, Great Gabâ! Am I the first here?"

The first of the gang to arrive pulled himself out of the undergrowth and made his way over to Dinky at the cave mouth.

"Yes, the others will be here in a minute. They have just sent me a text to say they are on their way. What would we do without our mobile phones, eh?" Dinky gestured to his phone, which was lying beside him and was nearly as big as himself. Soon the others appeared, dragging their mobile phones along as they went.

"Careful with those phones, please!" said Dinky. "They are not easy to come by, remember. Tourists are really careful with them and they are hard to steal."

"Sorry, boss," apologised a tarsier, whilst trying to stand his phone upright. "Are we ready to get started then?"

"Yes, I'm ready when you are. Come on, let's go inside. Cocoa doesn't last forever, you know."

The little gang got ready to carefully make their way over the loose rocks at the cave mouth. Their large nocturnal eyes quickly adjusted to the light in the gloomy interior. In silence, they followed Dinky in single file, those with mobile phones holding them carefully with long string fingers, deeper down into the cave system. After making their way along the treacherous, narrow, twisting passage that led down underground, they reached a small domed cavern. Here, a little spring bubbled and gurgled.

Beside the spring was a large pile of cocoa pods. They had all been freshly brought down by the tarsiers over the last few days. Those with phones put them down carefully in a pile, away from the trickling water. They would take the cocoa pods from the plantations where they were grown, and carry them through the forest to the secret cave. The tarsiers then took them down safely into the cave system, all without being seen by the increasingly abundant army of tourists.

Dinky's gang found that these phones were vital to coordinate their operations.

The process was ready to begin.

Dinky's father had been taught this special secret and it was taught to him by his father and by his father before him. The secret had been passed down through all the male heirs of the family for generations. It hadn't been his dad's time to go, Dinky thought. The older tarsier would still have had so much more to tell him.

Dinky was forced to find it out for himself, through trial and error, and that was why he had shared this burden with his close friends, his gang. He had needed lots of help.

Dinky had spread the Great Gabâ myth, a story that his grandmother had told him. It was a traditional island tale. He wanted to try to further protect his secret from those that became too nosey.

If people believed that the powerful Great Gabâ was behind any mysterious happenings, they might be scared away.

The only trouble was that, unbeknown to Dinky, the myth and the rumours had now got completely out of control.

Dinky felt like he needed some fresh air whilst he worked, but he also knew that there was a risk of seeing a tourist as it wasn't dark yet. The risk was small now that it was evening. Most of the visitors would be making their way back to their hotels.

Outside the cave entrance, Dinky and his gang stretched in the fading light. They congratulated each other on the task they had completed. Now was the time for the magic to happen.

"Shh!" cautioned Dinky.

They all listened. It was the tell-tale crunch of visitors' footsteps coming up the hill towards them.

"Not a sound!" Dinky whispered. "You are all quite camouflaged, especially in this low light, so just move quietly into the undergrowth, and freeze."

The gang did as they were asked, once they all understood the danger. The little clearing by the cave mouth became quiet again. Dinky heard a voice taking loudly.

"Awww! I wanted to see a tarsier!"

"Well," said a different voice, "we've seen the Chocolate Hills today and we'll just have to go to the sanctuary tomorrow."

He took a careful peek and saw a person and a

small dog walk up towards the little clearing. The light was beginning to fade.

The person threw his jacket down on the floor to sit on and the dog sat next to him.

Dinky noticed that the person's phone was sticking out of a jacket pocket.

The dog laughed and said, "Think about how much we've been using phones on this trip. What would we have done without them?"

Dinky saw them looking at the setting sun that was now very low on the horizon. It was casting everything in a warm orange light. The shadows lengthened. In some places, they were already turning from twilight dusky brown to dark black.

"It's beautiful!" the person exclaimed.

"I totally agree," the dog said. "But it's really not over yet. We are no nearer to finding out what this chocolate thing is all about, the criminal gang are still on the run, and we haven't found the Great Gabâ."

Dinky took a sharp intake of breath. Gabâ?

Despite the danger, Dinky couldn't resist the mobile phone, which was poking out of the jacket spread out on the floor. It looked like a good phone too.

He was hidden in the shadows but could see the glinting eyes of tarsiers across the clearing. The eyes were looking at him and he had their attention. Then Dinky pointed at the protruding mobile phone and received the 'thumbs up' response from his friends. They were all ready. He made his move.

Dinky quietly twisted off a small bunch of berries from the tree next to him, choosing his moment. First, stretching his little arm backwards, he launched the bunch high into the air, aiming for them to land just in front of the tourists. The falling berries would distract them whilst the gang made their move on the protruding phone. That was the plan anyway.

CHAPTER 21
TARSIERS

"What is that?" I shouted, seeing a small shape moving out of the bushes towards us. "There are two more. Look, they are making a grab for your phone!"

Jeff laughed as he bent down to pick up his jacket from the ground. "It's so sweet! It must be one of those tarsiers. It's no wonder we haven't seen one today. If they are nocturnal then we are only likely to see one at night."

"It's a shame that we can't see the Great Gabâ tonight too," I joked. "Look, all the tarsiers have frozen. It must be their defense mechanism, to freeze at the first sign of any danger. My, their eyes are wonderfully big. Aren't they so tiny, though?"

Jeff crouched down next to me now, so that he could get a better look.

"Hello, little fellow," he said. "You're very cute, aren't you?" Jeff reached a finger out towards the animal to gently stroke him.

"Hey!" shouted out one of the other tarsiers. "Show some respect, please! Don't you know who you are about to stroke? That, my friend, is the Great Ga—"

"Shut up!" said Dinky harshly. But it was too late.

I gave a quick intake of breath in surprise. "You weren't just about to say 'the Great Gabâ', were you?" I asked.

"Run!" shouted Dinky. But they were just too late. Jeff's hands were already close to Dinky. He now threw himself forward onto the ground, grabbing Dinky's little body and holding him aloft. Two other tarsiers had taken a pace forward but stopped as they turned their heads to see their gang leader captured. It wasn't long before the rest of the gang forlornly traipsed out of the shadows that they had been hiding in. They joined the gathering in the clearing.

"Put me down now! Put me down now!" demanded Dinky in a surprisingly loud voice. He hammered his little fists down on my person's hand as he spoke, wriggling to get free. "I am not a pet; I don't feel safe!"

"Oh, yeah, sorry," said Jeff apologetically. "Just let me turn around and then I can put you down carefully. Now stop! Please don't run away."

Dinky jerked himself free and turned towards the safety of the bushes.

"We've got something really important to ask you... Great Gabâ."

Dinky stopped, gave himself a little shake and brushed himself down. He stood up straight, dignity restored, and said more quietly, "Please don't ever do that again. I am not your pet; I am a free animal. Show me some respect."

The tarsiers stood around in a group and stared up at us with their large eyes, all about fifteen centimetres high, and all waiting for what we were going to say next.

"Erm... let's start again," I suggested. "Hello, I'm Ned and this is my person, Jeff. We are from England and we've come all the way to Bohol to see you, because we want to ask you about... well... chocolate."

It was properly nighttime now. The night sky above was full of stars, the like of which I'd never seen at home in England.

"Yes, I am the Great Gabâ," Dinky grandly admitted. "I am a chocolate expert. These other tarsiers are my loyal friends." He stopped then relaxed a little. "My birth name is Dinky, but if you are trying to create a living myth, of power, magic and magnificence, Dinky is not a very awe-inspiring name."

"I understand that," I said, bending my front legs quite low to the ground, so as to be on Dinky's level. "But why would you want to be awe-inspiring and magnificent? What are you doing?"

"Why do you ask?" Dinky became guarded once

more. "Why do you seek the Great Gabâ?" he said magnificently.

"Okay, Dinky, or Gabâ or whatever you prefer, let me tell you what we know. In England, there are lots of dogs, lots of packs of stray dogs, who are going around the country stealing old people's mobility scooters, crashing them through sweet shop windows and stealing all the chocolate."

"This is unfortunate," Dinky commented, fiddling with an insect, debating whether to start eating it or to continue talking. "What would dogs want with chocolate? Apart from rats and humans, animals are unable to eat chocolate, aren't they? It is poisonous to them."

"That's right!" chimed in one of Dinky's gang members. "It's the chemical in it called theobromine. It's toxic stuff! We overheard a conversation with a park ranger in the sanctuary. They were explaining to a tourist why they should not try to feed the animals with chocolate."

"That's right," I said. "Some of the dogs have made themselves very ill. They have been destroying chocolate by eating it." I held a paw across my stomach as I spoke, thinking of poor Rufus, who I had found sick in the park in Plymouth.

"And they have said," continued Jeff, "that it was you, the Great Gabâ, who was telling them to do it."

"What!" spluttered Dinky. His mouth was full of the insect, sending bits of chewed-up legs and wings shooting everywhere. "No, I have never heard anything so silly! I mean… I would never hurt another animal! Well, maybe just a… little, tiny… um…" He quickly hid the remains of the insect he was chewing behind his back. "But no! I would never tell animals to mess with chocolate. Did they explain to you why they were doing it?"

"Yes, they sort of did," I said. "They said that their lives were miserable at the moment. They are all stray dogs that have been abandoned and have to live on the streets. They said that the Great Gabâ has promised them hope, but first they would need to show their true loyalty for Gabâ by putting themselves in danger. They needed to steal chocolate. I know, it sounds silly, doesn't it? Especially when you say it out loud like that."

All the tarsiers started talking together at this latest news, with a babble of tiny voices.

"Stop!" Dinky ordered. "I need to find out more. Tell us, who is saying this rubbish to them?"

"It seems to be some kind of street gang leaders, or messengers as they call themselves. They are dogs that have come from somewhere else that are spreading all these rumours. The gangs are told that Gabâ hates humans and, by taking their chocolate, they are taking away some pleasure."

"He's sort of right, Dinky!" mumbled a tarsier with his mouth full. "You have always said how you really hate the people and you want your revenge on them, you know, for what they did to your father. That's what Gabâ means, doesn't it? Divine retribution."

"Oh dear!" exclaimed Dinky. "That sounds really

bad. Yes, I do hate human tourists coming to Bohol. Some of them caused the death of my father."

"Was it by trying to take him away from the island as a pet?" I asked.

"Yes, how did you know?" said Dinky, surprised. "But this whole story seems to have got mixed up by someone, and they are using it to steal chocolate. I can't understand the reason behind the robberies. They have nothing to do with me. I only care about Bohol, and… the great secret."

All the tarsiers turned their heads towards Dinky and shifted uncomfortably where they sat.

"I thought we weren't going to mention that, boss," said a tarsier, very seriously.

"What secret is this?" I asked.

"Come with us," said Dinky with a sigh, getting to his feet. "It's easier if I show you. Maybe I can help you to solve your mystery."

All the tarsiers rose and so did we. They started to waddle off towards the small cave.

Before entering, Dinky stopped and turned, addressing us very carefully.

"What you are about to see is a very, very big secret. I am showing you because it is important that you don't think we have anything to do with your poor stray dogs at home. They sound like they have been the victims of an enormous and terrible hoax. I am showing you so you can understand what we're really doing, and then you will see *why* we have done it. Prepare to be amazed."

CHAPTER 22
AMAZING!

Dinky turned and led us in single file down into the little cave. "Just keep to the path and follow us carefully," Dinky advised.

I could see where I was going quite easily. Dogs can see reasonably well in the dark. Jeff, however, was having terrible difficulty. He had to walk along by shuffling his feet carefully, one foot forward at a time. He bent down to avoid knocking his head on the tunnel roof. To make it worse, people can't see in the dark. Jeff used the torch on one of his phones to light his way. Dinky was very impressed.

"Nice phone," he said. "I didn't know phones have torches. Then again, with my nocturnal eyesight, I've never needed a torch."

Slowly but surely, we all made our way down

towards the spring, deep in the caves. The tunnel became complicated now. There were side passages that led off in all directions and gaping black holes that suddenly opened up above us in the ceiling. We could often hear the sound of gushing running water as we passed a dark opening in the wall. I tried to ignore these worrying underground dangers and just concentrated on the path in front of me. We had to trust this little tarsier that we had only just met, a tarsier who had admitted to us that he hated tourists.

Suddenly this didn't seem such a good idea.

As we got closer, it became easier to see, and Jeff stumbled and tripped less. The reason for this was a mysterious gentle glow that came from the cave ahead of us. The light became brighter and pulsed gently, although never becoming really bright. As we approached the end of our journey into the hill, we quickly came to see the reason.

It was the water. The clear water was bubbling from a small mound and then disappearing down a little rivulet, which led out of the other side of the cavern. The water itself had a bluish glimmer, as if it were lit from inside. There were one or two cocoa pods lying next to the spring.

The group of six tarsiers, plus one Jack Russell and one human, spread ourselves out in the cavern so that we were all facing the spring. In a hushed silence, we all stood waiting for an explanation.

Dinky stepped forward and picked up one of the cocoa pods with both hands. He stood next to the bubbling spring, in the centre of the group. The cocoa pod was nearly the same size as Dinky, standing with the pod upended on the floor, his little right arm resting on the top of it.

"This is where the magic happens," he announced. "There are many caves and springs underneath the Chocolate Hills, but only one spring like this."

"What does it do?" I asked, now very intrigued.

"First," he said, "answer me this. What is chocolate made from?"

"Cocoa pods," Jeff said. "Like the one you have there."

"Correct," said Dinky, pointing at Jeff as he said the word. "And do you like chocolate? Do you eat a lot of it?"

"I love it!" Jeff answered without hesitation. "And yes, I eat it at every opportunity. I especially like dark chocolate, except when there is a nice piece of milk chocolate on offer. Actually, I do really like white chocolate; I know that's not strictly chocolate because it doesn't really come from the cocoa pod, but I sometimes really like dark chocolate with sea salt. Yes, or with a soft filling, like caramel. In fact, I—"

"I get the idea!" interrupted Dinky. "But do you like chocolate, Ned, and do you eat a lot of it?"

"Well, I love the smell of chocolate," I answered. "And I would love to be able to eat it. But as with all animals, I can't, because it's really poisonous."

"Yes, and there lies the big problem!" Dinky let the cocoa pod fall as he waved both arms as he talked to us. "We animals just love the smell of chocolate, and normally, things that we like the smell of are okay to eat. Chocolate, however, naturally contains a substance called th...tho... oh, what's it called again?"

"Theobromine!" the gang member who had said it earlier yelled. "It's called theobromine, Dink... I mean, Great Gabâ!"

"Yes, theobromine, thank you," Dinky continued. "And there hasn't yet been any way found to remove this substance from chocolate. In fact, in people, it has quite a nice effect. People like it. But in animals, if they eat chocolate, it can kill them, make them ill. They have to be made to vomit so that it leaves their body, and vets try to flush it out. So the thing is, animals can't eat chocolate." At this point Dinky paused and looked around at all the different animals that were in the cavern.

"That is... until now!" he announced grandly, raising both of his arms into the air.

"But how?" I asked, astonished and excited by this news. "If this were true, this could mean that we could all eat chocolate. Whoever knew this secret would quickly become rich beyond their wildest dreams."

"Yes," Dinky agreed. "Very rich, very quickly, but everyone would want to know. Everyone would rush over here to Bohol and set up their factories and businesses. They would open loads of hotels and build roads and make theme parks for the visitors and... take over the whole island! Everything would change, and endangered species and precious rare environments would be spoilt and lost forever. Tarsiers would be taken. So no one must know. It must remain a secret."

"But, Gabâ," Jeff said quietly, "you haven't told us the secret yet."

"No, that is correct," agreed Dinky.

"Show them, Great Gabâ!" an excited tarsier shouted. "Yes, show them your secret; show them what makes you the one and only Great Gabâ!"

"Shh!" sharply hushed the others.

Dinky just nodded, then turned and picked up the fallen cocoa pod. He raised it high above his head and showed it to the audience, turning to face each one. Then he lowered his arms and turned to the spring. He carefully bent down and he pushed the cocoa pod down, under the surface of the water. All the watching tarsiers and Dinky counted aloud. "And one, and two, and three."

Dinky pulled up the cocoa pod and turned back to face us again.

"It is done!" he announced, nodding and smiling.

Personally, I was quite unimpressed. "What is done?" I asked. "All you have done is washed the cocoa pod off in the spring. Should we be impressed?"

Undaunted, Dinky now reached over into one of the dark cracks in the wall of the cave and pulled out some chocolate, carefully wrapped in dried banana leaves. He broke off some chunks, one of which he handed over to Jeff. One he put on a rock in front of me, and the other he held on to.

"After the count of three," Dinky instructed, "eat the chocolate. One… two… three!"

Jeff did not need asking twice and quickly wolfed down his chunk. Dinky too, ate his. I left mine on the rock in front of me. It smelt fantastic, though. My mouth was watering, but I knew that eating chocolate would make me ill.

"That," said Jeff, flinging his arms out in excitement and looking up towards the roof of the cave, "was the most amazing, the most delicious, the most mouthwatering, the most exciting piece of chocolate that I have ever tasted! It's like the chocolate of my most wacky, wildest, chocolatey dreams!"

Dinky smiled and the others tarsiers chuckled to themselves.

"You have not eaten yours, Ned," said Dinky. "Go on, eat it. Have you not eaten it because you think it will cause you harm? Well, I have eaten mine. Normally, chocolate is poisonous for us tarsiers too. Go on, try it. It's perfectly safe. I promise. You can trust me, Ned. I am the Great Gabâ that you have travelled so far to see."

My mouth was still watering, I was drooling now. It smelt divine! I really wanted to taste it. Surly a little piece would be okay?

"Go on, Ned," encouraged my person. "I trust him." And then, Jeff whispered to me behind his hand and out of the side of his mouth: "I noticed a vet just down the road that we passed on the way up. If the worst comes to the worst…"

"Ned," Dinky said in a serious voice, "that chocolate is made from cocoa pods that have been magically cleansed in the sparkling special spring of the Great Gabâ. The chocolate is now safe for animals to eat."

That did it, I would take a chance. I lunged forward to the chocolate chunk that Dinky had placed on the rock in front of me.

And my word, wasn't it incredible! It tasted ten times better than it smelt, and the texture in my mouth was the most wonderful thing I had ever experienced, so smooth and quick to melt.

The entire little group waited, looking at me for my reaction.

"Gabâ, you are indeed great!" I declared. "Even if I drop down dead in the next few minutes, it was all worth it. That chocolate was simply divine. It is quite safe for animals to eat, you say?"

"Oh yes," answered Dinky. "My father found out about this special spring years ago. It's incredible, isn't it?" Dinky beamed at me. "It means that even we animals can enjoy the wonders of chocolate! But you can't tell anyone," he pointed out, becoming serious now, "because that means that Bohol will be ruined by all of the visitors, by all of the animals wanting some of our chocolate, and by people trying to turn the secret into a business."

"Well," I said, after a few seconds of thought, "there certainly seems to be the possibility of making a lot of money here. Ah! Don't worry, Dinky; I won't tell a soul, your secret is safe with us. But I wonder if we could use the idea of becoming very rich on Bohol as bait, to trap some certain criminals."

"Now that's an idea!" exclaimed Jeff. "It could be the bait that we need to trap the chocolate cheats, who would do anything for money. They needn't ever discover the real secret; we could just hint at something really special happening on Bohol."

"Hee hee!" I laughed. "I think you and I must have a little chat, Dinky. Then our next move would be to give the man behind the newspaper a call, and phone Gizzmo too. Let's see if we can set up a very special sort of meeting. Lead us all out now, please, our new tarsier friends! You just can't get a good phone signal down here."

CHAPTER 23
PLANS

Once outside the cave, everyone who had a mobile phone swapped numbers. Jeff and I reassured Dinky once more that his secret was safe with us.

Although it was dark and coming to the end of our day, for the nocturnal tarsiers, their day was just beginning.

"We will need to meet up here again tomorrow at a similar time," I said. "You and I have some planning to do. My idea, though, might bring the criminals quite close to your secret cave. Are you okay about that?"

"That's okay by me," confirmed Dinky. "You may trick them into coming to Bohol, but there is no reason that they will find out about the animal chocolate. It will give me real pleasure to carry out my divine retribution on those who deserve it. We are going off to find something to eat now. The evening is the time for insects."

"Talking of eating," I said, "I would hate to think that this would be the last time I get to taste your wonderful, magical chocolate."

"Just let me see what I can do," said Dinky, his little teeth flashing into a warm smile in the moonlight.

My person and I walked back down the hill to the road, whilst the tarsiers disappeared off into the tropical forest.

"Those tarsiers are cute, though," said Jeff. "We've got so much to tell Gizzmo and MI5. We've solved the case really, all in one night!"

"It's not over yet," I replied, jumping down off the low bank onto the road. "We need to catch those criminals first. I will need a bit of help, but I think I've got a bit of a plan. Do you know, the best thing for me this evening has got to be that chocolate. We were right to trust Dinky, or should I say, the Great Gabâ. I feel absolutely fine now; in fact, I feel better than fine. If he was wrong about his chocolate being safe, I'd have been feeling pretty ill already. That tasted absolutely amazing. I wonder if he'll be able to send us some when we are back in England. Gizzmo would love it too."

"What do you think about this beautiful environment being destroyed by thoughtless people?" Jeff asked, as we made our way down the dry and dusty dirt track road.

"I think Dinky is quite right to be so careful," I replied, weeing on a roadside bush.

"Hey, if your plan to catch the criminals works," Jeff said, "how are we going to make sure that the people of Britain get their chocolate back? The criminal gang's plans are already in action. If anyone eats some of that Choccy Yum, like I nearly did, they are going to want even more."

"But don't you remember the meeting back in Hong Kong?" I replied. "They gave Boris some prune juice to cure him of the addiction. If they announce it all on the telly, along with the dangers of Choccy Yum, then that should solve the problem, I think."

But what would MI5 think?

CHAPTER 24
ROYAL CORGIS
SAY YES

"Well, what do you reckon, will it work?" I finally asked Gizzmo as I lay on the hotel bed, with Jeff's phone propped up against a complimentary jar of cashew nuts.

Gizzmo was in the little café again as she listened. I could just see the rim of her wide cup of Flat Bright in the corner of the picture.

"There are miles of treacherous caves under the Chocolate Hills that would be a danger for careless explorers," I observed. "I told you that the taxi driver said some people went down them after the Japanese gold. This could be the trap we need to bring all the criminals together. Dinky and his gang have some specialist cave knowledge that can help."

"Hey, dude, dude, dude!" Gizzmo was getting excited, or at least as excited as she could ever be bothered to get. "That sounds like a cunning type of plan, and the MI5 dude with the newspaper, is he able to do the business, you think?"

Jeff called over from beside the bed where he was listening. "Yes, he said he thinks it's a sure thing, 'A1' apparently."

Jeff was admiring his false moustache in the full-length mirror that was screwed to the wall. He kept tweaking the pointy ends of it as he spoke, and turned sideways to look from a different angle.

"He said," I confirmed, "that he will be in touch with his contacts around the world, and that messages will be sent. You've got Dinky's phone number now, haven't you, so you'll be able to sort out arrangements with him."

I sat up now with my paws in front of me and made room for my person as he sat on the bed, so that he could see Gizzmo too. Jeff was still scruffy, I thought, despite his disguise.

"Hey, no worries, dude," said Gizzmo. "You do your bit of the plan and we'll all do ours. MI5 will let us know when it's due to start, I guess. Hey, the bit that I'm most excited about is the chocolate; it's chocolate that we animals can eat! Tell me all about it; describe what it's really like, Ned, dude. Does it really taste as good as it smells?"

After our chat with Gizzmo, we both settled down to sleep. Neither of us slept very well. I was tossing and turning. I just couldn't stop thinking about chocolate and the plan to capture the criminals. Questions kept on going through my mind. What if they didn't take the bait? What if they realised that it was a trick and my plan had put us all in danger? I could tell Jeff was feeling nervous too. He got up to go to the toilet three or four times in the night, which was always a sure sign that something was worrying him.

At last, morning came, as did the news that we'd been waiting for.

Jeff answered the video call at almost the same moment that his phone began to ring and vibrate.

We held our breath in anticipation as the familiar newspaper came into view. This time with a different headline, I noticed: *A Prune Juice a Day Keeps the Choccy Yum Away*! it said.

"Morning, chaps," greeted a familiar voice. The man behind the newspaper flapped the newspaper once to pull it tight, and I got a little glimpse of a bit more of his hat, just for a second.

"As you can tell from the news headlines, the prune juice works rather well. The government is distributing free rations of it to everyone. Even if people aren't addicted to Choccy Yum, prune juice is jolly good for you. It's part of your five-a-day."

I smiled at this but was glad that I wasn't home in England at this moment, having to drink prune juice.

"Well, I can tell you officially," he went on, "after speaking to Larry the cat and the Prime Minister last night, it's on! Your plan has been approved and messages have already been sent out." He cleared his throat and said in very hushed important tones, "And that's not all. The Royal Corgis and their person, Her Majesty, have wished you all good luck. They have asked me to say to you that it is a wonderful thing that you are doing for your country. Hmm, so there."

"Wow!" I exclaimed, jumping up and shaking excitedly. "That is *soo* cool." I said this in my best Gizzmo voice. "When do we start?"

"The messages were only sent out a few hours ago and we are carefully tracing each of the criminal gang members. We know of their exact whereabouts. At the moment, they all appear to be in different countries. It's still all very hush-hush, of course, but in my opinion, those criminal gang members are all so greedy and determined to do anything that could make them rich, it won't be long before they are on the move. So just be ready, we'll let you know as soon as we know. Be prepared."

"What about the messengers that went around Britain, spreading all those rumours about the Great Gabâ? Gizzmo found out that they were trained out of the country, so that they wouldn't be detected."

"She was bang-on with her info," the man behind the newspaper confirmed. "Gizzmo makes a jolly good spy; her information is tickety-boo. We at MI5 have offered her a permanent job. Oh yes. Because of her work, we have been able to identify most of those troublemakers who have been hiding in our communities. One of them threw those underpants into your garden. The police are busy rounding them up as we speak. You'll be pleased to hear that help is also being given to the packs of homeless dogs." He ended the call.

"This is all turning out to be a very big operation," Jeff said. "Perhaps we could convince Rufus of the truth. He could then get a team together and go around de-brainwashing other dogs." Jeff looked at his watch. "We should get up and dressed – I mean, *I'll* get up and dressed."

"Yes, good idea," I agreed. "I think I'll just go outside to the toilet. There's no animal toilet in this hotel. Then I'll sit here and… look at the amazing view from our window."

"You can refresh your fur dye," Jeff reminded me. "We are in disguise, remember?"

It wasn't long before we were both ready to go. We sat on the bed and, whilst I licked between my claws, Jeff tapped his foot, feeling tense. We sat silently, both with a feeling of jumpiness in our tummies as we thought about what was happening. Even the Royal Corgis knew about my plan, wow!

"So, let's just go over this one more time," Jeff said. "MI5 have arranged for messages to be sent out to the criminal gang members, each message with their secret 'Three Dog Biscuits' picture on. That's the secret code that means that they won't be suspicious."

"Good thing we heard about that code," I said. "Otherwise, they might smell a rat."

"Yes, you have a good memory, Ned; we heard that when we were in the cellar in Brick Lane. The messages are instructing them to come here, to the Chocolate Hills, with all speed, if they want a chance at being the first to get to the newly discovered Japanese gold."

"That's correct," I confirmed. "The taxi driver told us about that gold. We have to make sure they go up to the right cave entrance. It has to be the cave that Dinky and his friends have organised."

"And," Jeff continued, this time pacing backwards and forwards around the room as he spoke, "they won't recognise us, as we are pretending to be taxi drivers who are waiting to take them from the airport to the Chocolate Hills. We'll be in our amazing disguises!"

"That's the scary part," I said, now jumping down from the bed to walk around beside my person as he paced around the room. It felt better to be walking about. "I think our disguises will be enough, because they have never really had a proper look at us anyway. There was that one time as we were coming out of the Ritz-Carlton building in Hong Kong where they became suspicious. But we'll just have to risk it."

"There's a bit I don't yet understand," said Jeff, standing still for a moment to look properly at me. I turned to look up at him too. "What happens when the criminals are in the caves... because why they can't..."

We both froze as we heard the phone ringing.

"Answer it then!" I exclaimed, looking at Jeff, who was still standing there, frozen.

"Oh yes," he said quickly, in a high-pitched voice. He suddenly came back to life and grabbed the ringing phone. It was the man behind the newspaper.

"The blighters are greedier than we first thought," he informed us. "They are already on their way and we have had reports that some are in Manila. It's only about an hour's flight to Bohol so you had better look smart and go now! Good luck. Whatever happens, we will remember that you did your duty..."

CHAPTER 25
THE MARVELLOUS NEDMONDO

We went! As fast as we could, we pelted down the stairs, slamming the door shut behind us. I ran across to the old taxi that we had been able to borrow from the taxi driver. He had said that if we borrowed it, we must be very careful and promise not to scratch it. We needn't worry about locking it, because the locks did not work anyway.

Jeff was not far behind me and he leaned over and opened the creaking taxi door. It already had lots of old scratches on it. I jumped in. Jeff got into the other side and after a few goes, started the engine.

"Did the taxi driver not mind us borrowing his

car?" I asked as we drove along the dusty potholed track that led towards the airport.

"Not at all," Jeff replied. "Well, definitely not when I waved a big wodge of that money we've got. He said that was more than he would earn in a month!"

As we rumbled along the dusty road, I started to feel nervous again and fidgeted in my seat.

"It's Boris that I'm most worried about," I said. "If he recognises us, or the other criminals set him on us, then we are in real trouble. He is a very big and strong dog. Besides, the others might have guns. They've already tried to kill us twice."

"We must just trust in our disguises and appear confident," Jeff reassured me. "At least you have an exciting name when you are in disguise, Nedmondo! My name is just plain old John. Ah, we're nearly there now. It's just in here."

We turned off the main road and into Tagbilaran Airport.

"I can think of lots of famous people called John," I commented, trying to keep our minds on less worrying things. "See if you can park where the taxi picked us up when we arrived. That's where they are expecting to meet us."

I looked around at the airport buildings. No flight had landed yet and the place did not seem very busy. We were all ready for them. I gave my false moustache a final check in the mirror and admired my newly reapplied fur dye. They would never recognise me, at least not by looks. These were dogs that we were dealing with, though, so I had made the effort to find something smelly to roll in outside the hotel. For dogs, smell is one of the first things that we would notice.

We both turned and looked at each other when we could hear the sound of an aeroplane in the distance. This could only be them.

"Remember when we flew in," I said. "It didn't take long to get from the aircraft and out through the airport terminal. This is an internal flight in the Philippines, and they won't have to go through loads of security when they get off. Also, they go down steps from the aeroplane onto the runway. Let's be ready."

Jeff took a firm hold of the steering wheel as if to brace himself. I sat and stared at the glass front doors of the terminal building, looking inside for the approach of our special visitors.

Here they came. Mr Yan led the way. He was looking businesslike in his suit, his bald head gleaming in the sunlight. Mr Yan was striding ahead purposefully, holding open the doors for the dainty and pretty Bichon Fraise, Princess Gem. Behind her strutted the smart Italian Greyhound, Carlos Fandango, and bringing up the rear, always checking around him suspiciously, was the big and beefy dark form of Boris Chuggworth.

Mr Yan spotted our taxi, waved to the others, and they all made their way towards us.

Mr Yan went straight around to the boot, opened it and slung his small black suitcase inside. He slammed the boot shut, whilst the others all piled onto the back seat. Mr Yan squeezed in beside them.

"No-a one told us dare were two of you!" Carlos whinnied. "I always like-a to sit up in de front."

"Very sorry, sir!" I turned around and answered. "Our driver today doesn't speak very good English, so I came along to act as your guide and answer any questions."

"It's okay," Princess Gem said calmly. "We all fit in just fine. Now off we go, please. I'm very eager to see all this gold. I've heard it's fabulous!"

"Oh yes, Miss," I replied. "You won't be disappointed."

We trundled out of the airport and onto the road. The windows of the taxi were all open to let the warm breeze cool everyone down.

"Is there lots of gold?" Mr Yan asked. "I've heard there is. That's why I came in such a hurry. I wanted to make sure that no one else got their thieving hands on it."

"Oh yes, sir," I replied, turning completely around in my seat, with my paws up on the back of the headrest. "There is tons of it, literally. The Japanese, who left it there, had stolen lots from all the countries that they invaded in the Second World War. They hid it all in a cave. It's a complete treasure trove!"

All the passengers on the back seat looked at each other in delight. Even Boris allowed himself a smile.

"Dis is-a good news," whispered Carlos to the others, "because dey have announced de 'prune juice cure' on-a the telly-box. Someone has revealed our plans. We need-a dis gold."

Princess Gem turned her head to give Carlos a very dirty look at this news that their wicked plan was beginning to unravel.

"Who found the gold?" she asked. "And why are they not keeping it and becoming fabulously rich?"

"It's because of the legends and the local traditions, Miss," I replied. "It was found by local animals and they think of these caves as being sacred and special. They won't touch anything they find in there, as it would be bad luck."

"I get it," Boris growled. "But why aren't *you* taking it then? And why are you telling us about it?" He paused. "You look like someone I know. 'ave we met before?"

I felt my stomach lurch. I had to keep my cool.

"We are just loyal servants of the Great Gabâ," I explained. "As, I'm sure, are you."

The passengers on the back seat all looked at each other rather sheepishly; Mr Yan even looked guiltily down at his feet.

"Oh yes, of course!" Princess Gem agreed. "Yes, of course this is all for the Great Gabâ. We are just going to take all of the gold away, to look after it for him."

"Yes, yes!" everyone on the back seat chorused.

"Of course, Miss. Well, we are nearly there now, just a little way along this bumpy track."

Jeff followed the directions to the cave mouth

which Dinky had given us. It was a cave that Dinky and his gang had prepared.

We slowed to a creaky stop, in a cloud of dust. The cave entrance could just be made out through some bushes beside us.

"Here we are," I said. "We are in Bohol's famous and beautiful Chocolate Hills area. If you look up—"

"Yes, yes, very nice, I'm sure," interrupted Carlos as he jumped out of the car. Mr Yan, who had already got out, yanked the creaky door open for him. "Now will you please show us the piles of gold?"

"Of course!" I said jauntily, jumping down from the old taxi myself. "Are we all ready? Yes? This way, please. Follow me."

Out of the corner of my eye, I caught a little quick glint of light in the shadows. I coughed loudly to cover the rustling sound of the tarsiers, moving further away out of sight into the lush green bushes.

I stopped next to Jeff as we stood at the cave mouth. He was holding back the bushes that grew over the entrance, revealing a dark roundish hole. It was tall enough for Mr Yan to walk into, only stooping slightly.

"Now please notice," I said, whilst Jeff handed a lit candle to Mr Yan, "there are lots of bats in this particular cave, and we really don't want to frighten them. Besides, they do make a horrible pooey mess if disturbed. That's why you have only got one candle to see by. We don't want to wake them up."

"Oh no, of course," agreed Princess Gem. "We don't want them making a mess on my lovely white fur!"

"Your eyes will soon get used to the dark," I continued, moving away from the cave mouth myself, to let the eager treasure hunters get nearer. "There is so much gold; you really can't miss it."

"Ooh!" Carlos said in excitement. "Well let's-a get to it den. I'm-a going to be rich!"

"Yes!" shrieked Princess Gem in delight. "We are going to be in control of all the world's chocolate with our amazing Choccy Yum plan, and now we have huge amounts of gold too! I know you've got the candle, Mr Yan, but if I could just squeeze past… Oh, what's this? Look. There is some gold already just by the entrance. There must be lots more!"

That's a nice touch, Dinky, I thought. Give them a little taste to get them excited by placing shiny gold near the entrance. Even I could see that it was a cheap gold-coloured plastic ornament. The criminals were so excited now that they didn't look properly.

It worked, though. Pushing to get past each other and be the first to the gold, the group squeezed themselves through the cave entrance, as they all tried to get in at once.

"Oh-a wow!" I heard an Italian-sounding voice say. "'ere's a bit more."

This new find, yet again arranged by Dinky, kept them pushing even further into the cave.

The bushes rustled and out came the little figures of Dinky and his gang. They were all trying to stay in the shadows of the leaves, as they would not usually come out in the daytime.

"It's working," said Dinky. "They are going deeper into the cave system. We just want them to keep going a little more… I picked this cave very carefully, of course… and it should be about now… and… ooh, I can't wait… and…"

Then there was silence. We could no longer hear the clamour and shrieking of excited voices. There was nothing.

We all stood by the cave mouth and looked at each other. Dinky turned his head to look up at us with his huge eyes and smiled. "Don't feel too sorry for them," he said. "I am the Great Gabâ after all." He paused. "I give divine retribution."

Jeff and I looked at him, waiting for an explanation as to what had happened to the chocolate cheats.

"It serves them all right for being so greedy," Dinky explained, shrugging his little shoulders, as if to excuse himself. "And for making all those poor dogs so ill, by eating all that chocolate. Well, now that can all stop. The Great Gabâ has spoken!" he said in a dramatic voice, holding his little fists up in the air. Dinky then chuckled; his gang all chuckled too.

"What exactly has happened to them?" I asked, feeling a bit concerned now. "My plan was just to trap them in one of the Bohol caves. I thought that we were just tricking them all to go in, because they thought they would be getting rich. I hadn't planned to…"

Dinky laughed again. His gang giggled.

"Don't you worry," he said. "They are not dead or anything, just a bit wet and cold, and unable to get out without help. Their help is coming in a minute in the form of MI5 and Interpol. They are coming here to arrest them."

"But I heard all their voices suddenly stop, like they had disappeared!" Jeff said, rather alarmed.

"That's because," explained Dinky, "they fell down a deep hole into some very cold water! These caves can be very treacherous, you know. There are lots of little surprises and things to watch out for. Cave exploring should only be done by those that know what they are doing."

"I guess they do deserve a bit of a nasty surprise!" I gave the little tarsier a gentle lick of appreciation. I allowed myself a smile as I imagined them all in the dark, cold and dripping wet, standing in a pool up to their knees. "And here come MI5 and Interpol. Their cars have just pulled up. So I think we've successfully achieved this bit of my idea."

"Then your plan has succeeded," cried Dinky, saluting me in appreciation. "If I am known as the Great Gabâ, henceforth, you shall be known as the Nifty Nedmondo!" All the tarsiers murmured in agreement at this idea.

"It says Nedmondo on your passport, doesn't it?" said Jeff. "'Nifty Nedmondo' can be your spy name."

"You can all come back to my secret cave. It's not too far away from here," Dinky suggested. "We can celebrate with some CHOCOLATE!"

CHAPTER 26
AWESOMENESS

I lapped at the froth on my cup of Flat Bright, and looked up at Gizzmo with a little grin. "Go on, they are for you, try some," I suggested, using my nose to nudge the delicate wooden box across the table.

We were sitting at Gizzmo's usual place by the window in The Sticky Bun. I could smell the sea air of Plymouth and home. Jeff was slowly continuing to stir his coffee with a teaspoon; both our eyes were fixed on Gizzmo's reaction to her gift.

After saying our goodbyes to our new friends in Bohol, we had returned to Britain the same way that we had come. The criminal gang members had been arrested and brought back too. They had been given really long prison sentences and put into super secure prisons with armed guards, guarding them twenty-four hours a day.

We had stopped off in London to visit Noola on our journey home. We needed to pick up our car, and to say sorry that we hadn't been able to stay for very long. She had some of her special soup ready for us, and said that she knew we were coming home that day because the man behind the newspaper had knocked on her door and told her.

"He didn't put the newspaper down once," she said. "There was just one moment when he had to let go of one side, to quickly pass me this envelope, that I caught a brief glimpse of a very large bushy moustache. Then he caught hold of the newspaper again."

Jeff and I smiled at each other, our own moustaches now gone, and my fur back to its normal colour.

"He thanked me for my help and said that Larry, the Number Ten Downing Street Cat, sent me a little gift of appreciation too."

"And what was it?" Jeff asked, eagerly inquisitive.

"It's an invitation to dinner at Number Ten," she replied. "An award-winning Michelin Star soup specialist is cooking, and I am the guest of honour; I'm so thrilled!"

"Fantastic!" I exclaimed, scratching my ear with my hind leg. "I'm pleased for you, of course, but how come they invited you?"

"You'll never guess," Noola giggled, unable to stop smiling. "I've got a connection to Number Ten now.

Larry the cat has a sister, called Lavender. Lavender's person is really old and has had to move into a retirement home. Lavender is now coming to live here, with me!"

"That's really good news," said Jeff. "How did you find out that she was looking for a new house?"

"It was all arranged by the man behind the newspaper," Noola answered. "He regularly has to have important meetings with Larry, and it was just mentioned in conversation. I've wanted to share my house for a long time. Lavender is a traditional animal, and now I'll have the perfect housemate."

In The Sticky Bun, we told Gizzmo about Lavender, and explained the gift that was on the table.

"All the way home, from when Dinky said his goodbyes and gave us this little box, I have just been imagining your reaction the first time you taste it," Jeff said, still stirring his coffee. At last, he stopped stirring, and waved the spoon around instead as he spoke. "Yes, all the way back to Manila, then to Hong Kong and then back to London, I was thinking, how is Gizzmo going to react? Didn't I say that, Ned?"

"Yes, you did, many times," I replied, also eager for Gizzmo to open the box.

"I looked at that box, which I kept safely in my pocket, and I said to myself, this is going to be a special moment."

"This is so cool, dudes!" Gizzmo exclaimed. "And Dinky sent this back with you from Bohol especially?"

"He certainly did," I replied. "When I told Dinky all about you, and how you had helped us right from the start, he said, 'Gizzmo definitely deserves a little treat for all her efforts.'"

"Dudes!" said Gizzmo, taking a lap at her Flat Bright and staring at the little box. "This is just so awesome! Now that the members of the gang are all safely in jail, we can relax and chill."

She raised her paw up to the tabletop and held it just beside the box. "Here goes!" she exclaimed. "One experience of total awesomeness."

With that, she flipped open the little lid with a click, and we all leaned forward to stare at the contents. The smell that was released was, as Gizzmo would say, totally awesome. It took me straight back to that cave, when Dinky had offered me that first taste. Gizzmo scooped her paw delicately into the box and lifted out a little piece of the magical dark, creamy brown animal-friendly confectionery. She looked at it for two or three seconds, lifted it up to her little nose and closed her eyes. She took a long sniff.

Dinky had arranged that, for keeping his secret, he would post little boxes of his special animal chocolate. He would send one to me, to Gizzmo, to each of the Royal Corgis and to Larry the Number Ten Cat. He would send some every three months. The Royal Corgis were away at the minute on one of their worldwide tours, and they were now going to include Bohol.

"I think I'm going to like chocolate," Gizzmo said, grinning broadly and popping the small piece into her mouth. She smiled.

Just then, our celebrations were interrupted by the loud rustle of newspaper.

In front of us stood the man behind the newspaper, behind a newspaper. We all stopped what we were doing to look around at him.

"Sorry to interrupt, chaps. I think that we are going to need your help again. I've come down especially from London to see you in person. Now you have the security clearance, and we are officially making you a secret agent, Gizzmo, we'll need you to start immediately. It's a very delicate matter. You see, you remember that briefcase that Mr Yan put into the boot of the taxi, when you picked the criminal gang up from the airport on Bohol? Well, we've just managed to open it, and you'll never guess what we found inside…"